THE WHISKERED SPY

NIC SAINT

PUSS IN PRINT PUBLICATIONS

THE WHISKERED SPY

Copyright © 2013-2015-2019 by Nic Saint

All rights reserved. No part of this book may be reproduced in any form by any electronic or mechanical means including photocopying, recording, or information storage and retrieval without permission in writing from the author.

This is a work of fiction. Names, characters, places, brands, media, and incidents are either the product of the author's imagination or are used fictitiously. The author acknowledges the trademarked status and trademark owners of various products referenced in this work of fiction, which have been used without permission. The publication/use of these trademarks is not authorized, associated with, or sponsored by the trademark owners.

Edited by Chereese Graves

www.nicsaint.com

Give feedback on the book at: info@nicsaint.com

facebook.com/nicsaintauthor
@nicsaintauthor

First Edition

Printed in the U.S.A

FOREWORD

Back in 2013 I was a struggling writer and desperately casting about for a genre to write in (I didn't know I'd go on to write in every possible genre under the sun before I'd find a measure of success). I was proudly owned by a big red cat named Tommy and had been writing blog posts about him for a while. So I finally decided to write an entire book from his (fictitious) viewpoint. And so The Whiskered Spy was born, originally written and published as a three-part serial.

I wrote the serial between June and July 2013 and it was published in November that year under my real name. I moved to the Nic Saint pen name in 2014, still looking for a suitable genre to write in. It took until September 2015 before I tried my hand at cozy mystery with the first book in the Bell & Whitehouse series and a short while later decided to try a cat sleuth series, in the same vein as The Whiskered Spy but with more input from the humans, as writing a story solely from the viewpoint of a cat turned out to be a little tricky. After all, once the feline sleuths figure out whodunit, they can't exactly call the police to make the arrest.

And so The Mysteries of Max was born in August 2017.

Before that, though, I republished The Whiskered Spy under the Nic Saint pen name, as I hoped more readers than the precious few who'd enjoyed it the first time around would want to meet Max's forerunner, the original feline spy.

Since then many people have asked if there will be more books about Tommy, to which I can say that Tommy is enjoying his well-earned retirement now. The only clues he hunts these days involve finding the best spot in the house for taking naps, and figuring out what's for dinner. The real sleuthing he leaves to his cousin Max, who will go on to have many, many more adventures :).

Nic Saint, December 2019

THE BROOKRIDGE PARK HORROR

I was sitting in an elm tree looking down at the world below, minding my own business, when the stirring events I'm about to relate took place. As it happens, it was my favorite tree to sit and watch the world go by while licking any part of my anatomy that needed licking. Not that I'm a philosopher, per se. But I'm a cat and, closely following Chapter 3, Paragraph 6, Section 8 of the Cat Guild Book of Regulations, sitting in trees is a task highly recommended to fill at least one time slot a day, an average time slot equaling more or less 7 human hours. And it was as the last minutes of my tree-sitting time for the day were ticking away, that I became aware of strange happenings down on the ground below.

The perch I had chosen for my tree time was located in the middle of the Brookridge park, which has, among its many other points of interest, a very large population of birds that like to occupy its various trees—closely following the rules of *their* particular guild. And as everyone knows, chasing birds is clearly outlined in Chapter 1 of the Cat Guild rulebook as one of the mainstays of an adult cat's life.

But apart from cats, trees and birds, another life form habitually infests the Brookridge park: humans. And it were two members of this odd species who were now hobnobbing under my tree's foliage.

Clearly laboring under the misapprehension that they were alone, they were speaking in the hushed tones of the professional hobnobber. I pricked up my ears and studied the duo intently. One was a female human, oddly enough dressed up in white, as if preparing to attend a wedding, the other a male. And for a moment I had labeled their actions as part of the mating ritual humans like to observe: first they spend the longest time talking, then some form of physical contact follows, and finally they start locking lips, something I've never been able to endure with fortitude.

And I was about to hop to the next tree and save myself the sickening spectacle, when words reached my ears that perked me up considerably.

"I think he's on to us," said the female.

"Are you sure?" said the male.

No reply followed, but from the next sentence spoken by the male, it was obvious the woman had given him some form of nonverbal confirmation.

"That's too bad," he said. "That means we'll have to take him out."

I can tell you right now that my tail shivered from stem to stern at these words. 'Take him out'. That could only mean... Here, through some form of divine intervention, I had stumbled upon a secret meeting between two spies! I knew of course that Brookridge is a veritable nest of spies and its local park their favorite hangout, but it was the first time I'd ever encountered two real-life spies in the flesh. And under my favorite tree no less! Talk about ringside seats.

The woman gasped. "Take him out!" she said. It was

obvious to me that she didn't agree with her fellow spy's assessment of the situation. "Are you nuts?"

"Nuts about you," whispered the man. "And I'll be damned if I'm going to let that little weasel get in the way of our future happiness. Either he goes, or I go."

"No! Jack!" cried the woman. "Don't go!"

At these words, my tail stopped shivering and my ears flopped. This was not the talk of two spies planning to take out some unfortunate competitor, but of two lovers, plotting to do away with a husband or wife or possibly both. I heaved a deep sigh to signify the premature dashing of all my hopes and dreams and languidly trotted to the edge of the branch I'd been sitting on to prepare for my departure from the lurid scene. It no longer held any interest for me.

Unfortunately, just in that moment, another cat arrived on the scene and engaged me in conversation. It was Dana, the highly strung Siamese belonging to one of the neighbors.

"Hello, Tom," she said in her customary sultry voice. "What are you doing out so late? Don't you have to be home with daddy around this time of night?"

"Hi there, Dana," I said in my most casual way. "Where did you spring from all of a sudden?"

"Oh, I was just hopping around here and there, checking out the neighborhood, when I happened to run into Stevie. You know Stevie, don't you? Father Sam's Ragamuffin?"

Yes, I knew Stevie. The mongrel ate a mouse I'd marked for my own one night when I wasn't watching. "Shh," I said, for I noticed Dana's jabbering had interrupted the easy flow of conversation coming from the couple downstairs.

"Shh, yourself," said Dana, amused. "No one shushes me, Tom. You know that. As I was saying, I ran into Stevie and noticed he'd done something different with his whiskers. They seemed, I don't know, longer or something. So I said, 'Stevie. I like what you've done with your whiskers. What's your secret?' And Stevie said, 'Extensions. It's the new craze.' And I said—"

"Will you please be quiet!" I hissed. For my sensitive ears had picked up something else now. The woman had begun softly sobbing and the man was now whispering something consoling into her ear and patting her gently on the back. It wasn't this patting on the back that worried me, though, but the long and shiny butcher's knife he was pulling out of his pocket with his free hand and carefully poising behind the woman's back.

"Well, I never," said Dana, shocked at being spoken to like that by a mere tabby.

But then I directed her attention to the two people down below, and when she saw the moonlight glitter on the knife, she let rip a cry so piercing, it stayed the hand of the man just on the verge of plunging the knife into the woman's back. Both the man and the woman looked up to see what all the ruckus was about.

"He's got a knife!" trilled Dana.

I rolled my eyes at this piece of old news. "I can see that," I said. "And it looks like he's not afraid to use it."

"But then, he's a murderer!" cried Dana.

"Yah," I said. "Obviously."

"We have to stop him. Oh, Tom, do something!"

Now, humans habitually call for help on these occasions. Well, you're a human. You know the drill. You yell, 'Police! Help!', at the top of your lungs and more often than not someone will show up. Unfortunately, we cats can yell all we want but no police or help will show up. What we can do is cry our little hearts out, though, and if we're lucky, one of those fellows with a hard hat and a red coat will come running and save us from the tree. Firemen, I think humans call them. Exceedingly fine fellows I've always thought, and I'm on a first-name basis with most of Brookridge's finest.

"Let's pretend we're stuck in this tree and perhaps a fireman will show up," I said therefore.

"But why?" said Dana, frowning confusedly. "We're not stuck in this tree."

"I know we're not stuck in this tree, but that woman down there is going to get it in the neck if we don't do something quick!"

Her eyes lit up with the dim light of intelligence. "Oh, I see. We yell for help and when one of those nice red men show up, the killer will think twice about doing whatever he—"

She didn't finish her sentence for she had happened to glance down and I saw every thew and sinew in her slender body stiffen with apprehension. Following her gaze I started. The woman was now lying facedown on the grass, the man standing over her with the knife still in his hand. He was cleaning it methodically with a large handkerchief.

MURDER IN THE PARK

"*He* did it!" cried Dana. "He murdered that poor, poor woman!"

I wanted to point out that for all we knew the woman had simply decided to take a nap, the man preparing to butter a piece of toast for when she woke up, but it was obvious Dana was right for a change: a murder had taken place and we were both eyewitnesses.

"Dang," I said, as I stared my eyes out at the murder scene. It doesn't happen every day that you see a murder take place. Now, mind you, we hadn't actually seen 'it' happen, more like the before and after. But it wasn't hard to imagine what had happened in between. When you see a fellow raise a knife behind a woman's back and next thing you know the woman is lying lifeless on the ground and the man is cleaning the knife, the thing speaks for itself.

Dana, who was sobbing for dear life, suddenly turned on me with a vengeance. "It's all your fault," she cried. "If you hadn't started blabbing on and on about firemen, we could have saved that poor woman."

"Huh?" I said, too stunned to construct a decent retort.

Dana wrung her paws. "I should have simply jumped down on that awful man's back, claws extended. He wouldn't have been so eager to go sticking knives in innocent women's backs then. Or perhaps I should have jumped on his head and clawed at his nose. God knows I've done it before. Works like magic every time."

I shivered, and this time it wasn't from the sight of the gruesome scene down below, but from a slight apprehension at finding myself within striking distance of Dana's claws. I'm a big boy and I pride myself on my powers of self-defense, but when I encounter dames of Dana's obvious level of ferociousness, I respectfully bow out.

I started to do so now, but Dana stopped me with word and gesture. The gesture being a tap on my head and the word a menacing growl.

"Where do you think you're going?" she said.

"Ouch," I said, and rubbed the spot where she'd tapped me. "Home. Where else?"

"Home?" she cried, visibly appalled. "How can you talk about going home with this murder going on right under our noses. We have to…"

I gave her a wry smile. "We have to what? There's nothing we can do. The police will take care of everything."

"But, we know who did it. We can help the police."

I scoffed. "We're just cats. We can't help the police. We can't do a single thing."

"But, but…"

"I'm going home," I said, and turned to leave.

A searing pain in my left buttock made me change my mind. "On second thought…" I said, and watched as Dana licked her claws.

"We can't let murderer boy get away with this," Dana said. "Stevie would never…"

"Oh, please," I said. "Not Stevie again. That bird-brain

7

wouldn't do a single thing."

"Oh, yes, he would," said Dana, adamant. "Stevie's got more courage in one whisker than you have in that gruesomely large body of yours."

"My body isn't gruesomely large," I said, slightly offended.

"Yes, it is," she said. "We don't call you Fat Tom around the neighborhood for nothing."

"No one calls me Fat Tom," I said, appalled at the slur.

"We do, you know," said Dana with a smirk that didn't become her.

"For your information, I'm not fat," I said as haughtily as I could. "I'm just big, that's all. Large bone structure, Zack always says." Zack Zapp is, as the vernacular goes, my owner. Though I might as well add that no one really owns me, as I'm a free spirit. Well, that is until my stomach starts making funny noises and it comes time to have a stab at the cat bowl and find out what's for lunch.

"Then Zack is as big a chump as you are," Dana said decidedly. "Now, what are you going to do about that murdering fellow downstairs?"

"Nothing," I said, after throwing a glance at the ground floor. "Because he's legged it."

Dana, after ascertaining my observation was correct, frowned thoughtfully. "And so did she."

I did a double take at these words. It doesn't often happen that dead bodies get up and take off. Looking again, I saw that she was right: both the killer and the killee, if that's the word I want, had removed themselves from the scene.

"That's odd," I remarked. "Usually on these occasions the corpse stays put."

"Unless the killer took it with him."

"As a souvenir, you mean?"

Dana sighed. "Stevie was right about you. You really are a dumb brick."

"I am not! Humans often take souvenirs. When Zack came back from England he brought a pipe and a tea pot."

"A dead body is not a tea pot, Tom."

I had to admit she had a point there. At least a tea pot serves some purpose, no matter how small, whereas a dead body is of no use to anyone.

She reflected. "The killer is obviously trying to hide the body. Would you recognize him when you saw him again?"

I said I probably could. For when the fellow had looked up I'd taken a good look at his face. Nothing to write home about, mind you. Just one of those average human faces. Fortunately for me—Dana was extending those claws of hers once more—I'd spotted one distinguishable feature about the killer's face: a pimple.

"He had a large pimple on the tip of his nose," I said triumphantly as I kept a close eye on Dana's paws. "Unless it was a fly temporarily using the man's face as a launching pad." I gave a hearty laugh at my own joke. Dana didn't laugh.

"A killer with a pimple," she said. "And a dead body that has suddenly disappeared. Right." She got up and started threading her way down the branches of the tree.

"Hey, where are you going?" I said. For, though I was feeling relieved to finally be rid of her, I was also a bit peeved at the abruptness of her departure.

"I'm going to get help," she said, without looking back.

"Help? From whom?" Perhaps it should have been 'who', but whatever it was, Dana didn't deign to reply. The night swallowed her up and before long she was gone.

I shrugged and after having given the matter some more thought—do teapots really have more use than a human corpse? After all, a human body can be used as compost, whereas a teapot merely serves as an eyesore—I trotted off myself. A midnight snack and a warm bed were awaiting me and a tall tale to tell my friends bubbled on my lips.

THE THIRD DEGREE

J'd pretty much forgotten all about recent events, when a bark arrested my progress towards the homestead. It was Frank, the neighborhood watchdog. I know, watchdog isn't much of a way to describe any dog, but it's how we like to call him around these parts. Frank is in fact a Poodle—complete with woolly coat and docked tail— and fancies himself something of a local law enforcement officer. In other words, our very own flattie.

"Evening, Tommy," he said in his customary gravelly voice.

"Evening, Frank," I said, refusing, as usual, to address him as 'officer', something he's quite keen on.

"I just met Dana," he said, and cocked an inquisitive eye at me. I didn't take the bait and he continued. "She said she was a witness to some funny business happening in the park just now and you were also present at the scene. Care to comment?"

I sighed. So this was the help Dana had gone and found. "Yes, Frank," I said curtly, for what I wanted more than anything was to go home and have a bite to eat. Kibble and a bowl of milk awaited me. "I saw one human slash another human and then make off with the body. And no, I really don't think it is any of our business. If humans want to slay each other, fine. As long as they don't start in on any of our kind, I really don't see why we should get involved."

Frank waggled his ears. "Oh, so that's how you see it, is it?"

"That's how I see it, Frank," I said. As long as the humans keep the kibble coming, of course, but I didn't voice this thought to the self-appointed keeper of the peace.

"Well, now," he said, with a hint of reproach. "Isn't that kind of selfish?"

"No, it is not," I assured him.

"Then let me ask you this," he said. "What if that woman who'd just been brutally murdered was Zack? How would you feel about the situation then?"

I hate to admit it but the fluffy one had a point there. Apart from the fact that Zack was a man and not a woman, I probably would have felt differently if he'd been the one on the receiving end of the knife just then. "Well..." I said, trying to come up with something glib and witty.

"I thought so," Frank said with a grunt of satisfaction. "Selfish to a degree; that's the Tom I know."

"I'm not selfish," I protested, but I knew he had me licked. It's not just that Zack provides me with all the necessaries like food and shelter, I'm also quite partial to the way he tickles me under my chin and strokes my whiskers. And the way he fluffs up my pillow each time before I take a nap is also one of those things that endears him to me in ways that I find hard to describe to anyone but my closest friends. I do believe he loves me, if you catch my drift, and I have to admit to being quite fond of the big oaf as well.

"Look, that's neither here nor there. The fact of the matter is that Zack is not the one going around being stabbed in parks at night. He's too smart to ever get himself entangled with a cold-blooded murderer like that. And for one thing, the woman was cheating on her husband, so..."

Frank cocked an eye. "And that makes it all right for her to be whacked by some psycho in the local park?"

"No, that's not what I meant," I said quickly. Oh, boy, I really was sinking deeper and deeper into the quagmire. Perhaps I should just shut my big mouth and move on before I really got myself into trouble with the furry arm of the law. "What I meant was that..." To tell you the truth, I didn't really know what I meant.

"Right," said Frank. "Not only selfish to a degree, but also sexist. I see."

"Look, I understand the desire to make a character study of my person, but don't you have something better to do? Like to search for men with pimples on the tips of their noses? I'm sure Dana told you about that telling detail?"

Frank nodded, his ears flopping to and fro as he did. "She did, indeed. But I was hoping to extract some more details from you. Like what kind of clothes was he wearing? What color was his hair, his eyes, his face? Was he tall? Small? Fat? Skinny? What did he smell like?"

On and on the interrogation went. I supplied the good Poodle with all the details I could remember and finally, after what seemed like an interminable delay, I was finally released from Frank's scrutinizing gaze, and allowed to go on my merry way.

It still puzzled me a great deal why this self-appointed upholder of the law would go to all the trouble of conducting a police investigation in what clearly was a human affair, when my progress towards the kibble trough was halted once again. By then I'd reached the edge of the park and was trotting down the sidewalk, having once more managed to relegate the sordid details of the recent affair to the back of my mind.

A sudden hiss arrested my attention, and when I turned to verify its source, I found myself staring into the eyes of Brutus, my nemesis, staring back at me from the shrubbery.

4

MEET THE BULLY

*B*rutus, as you may or may not know, is the Persian belonging to Royce Moppett, Zack's next-door neighbor, and between us a warm enmity had sprung up from the first time we met. I don't know what it is about Brutus, but apart from the fact that he's a mean-spirited, bullying nosy parker, I guess I simply don't like him. And the feeling was obviously mutual.

"Hey, fattie!" he now hissed from the shrubbery.

Not deigning to respond to this insulting salutation, I continued on my way.

"Hey! Meatball!"

Turning a deaf ear, I held my tail up high, and pranced away. Unfortunately, before I had proceeded ten feet, the menace had joined me and fallen into step at my side.

"Why don't you listen when I talk to you?" he said plaintively, as if I had done him an injustice.

"Oh, you were talking to me, then?" I said, feigning surprise. "Well, seeing that my name is Tom—Tommy for my closest cronies—and not 'fattie' or 'meatball', I just assumed you were talking to yourself again. You do have a habit of soliloquizing, you know."

"Wise guy," Brutus said in a low voice. "I wanted to talk to you, Tommy." Somehow he always managed to pronounce my name as if it was a dirty word.

"No one is stopping you, Brutus."

"What's all this I hear about you reporting a murder in the park?"

I rolled my eyes at this incorrect representation of the facts. "For one thing, I never reported any murder. Who's been feeding you lies? One of your loathsome friends?"

Brutus has the most abhorrent circle of cronies. A bunch of repellent yes-cats that answers to his every beck and call as if he were the leader of a gang of sorts. Which, now that I come to think of it, he probably is.

"I got it from Ricky," he growled, "who got it from Rufus, who got it from Candy, who was there when Dana told the whole story to Frank, that wannabe copper. Some dame got whacked and you and Dana were there when it happened, and saw the whole thing."

I admitted to having been an eyewitness to the events he'd just described, but made strong objection to the use of the term 'whacked'. Frank's words had really rung a bell with me and I'd now come to consider the woman being murdered with the proper compassion she undoubtedly deserved.

Too true, I now saw, that being unfaithful is no reason to find oneself on the receiving end of a very large and very sharp knife. If everyone who has ever cheated on his wife or husband would meet with the same fate, the world would probably be a lot less populated than it is now.

"Now, tell me something. Was it a big knife?" said Brutus, his eyes gleaming with a strange light.

"I—"

"Was there a lot of blood? Did it spout from the vic like a geyser?"

"I really—"

"Is it true that the killer licked the knife clean? And that he howled like a werewolf when the light of the full moon lit up his savagely contorted face; half human, half beast?"

"Oh, please," I said, disgusted. Somewhere between Candy, Rufus and Ricky, the story had obviously taken a turn for the fantastic. Cats will be cats, and embellishments will find their way into any tale they tell. "Nothing of the kind. What do you think this is, Werewolf High? All Dana and I saw was some guy stab some woman and do a disappearing act with the mortal remains. No licking or howling was involved."

Brutus seemed disappointed. "You always were a spoil-sport," he grunted, indicating he held me personally responsible for ruining a perfectly good story by telling the truth.

"Look, I don't see what the big deal is," I said. "They're humans. They're prone to violence. They're not as level-headed and intelligent a species as we are and they will go around causing all manner of murder and mayhem. It has happened before and it will happen again."

"Not in Brookridge Park, it hasn't," said Brutus. "Frank said this is the first time something like this has ever happened around here."

"Oh, puh-lease," I said. "And what about that girl who fell from a tree last fall? Broke her neck and died on the spot."

"Accidental death," said Brutus with a touch of wistfulness. "Not a killer in sight, not even a small one."

"Or the boy who fell through the ice on the Brookridge Park pond? Didn't he die?"

"No, some idiot dove in and saved him. And, again, no one pushed him. He fell in all by his idiot self. No, this really is the first time a real, juicy murder has happened in this

16

little nook of the world, and you and Dana were the only ones to see it." He eyed me with the green eye of jealousy. "Of all the cats... And to think I would have been there if not for Ricky getting his tail entangled in those nasty bridge-side brambles."

Brutus had touched on a point of much contention between us. "That elm tree is mine, Brutus, and you know it."

"Trees don't belong to anyone, fathead."

"Well, that one does and everyone knows it. Don't you ever stop and smell the bark?"

"I do, and then I take a leak right on top of it."

It was true. No matter how many times I'd cordoned off my territory, this ugly-looking brute always managed to trespass and pee all over my scent. And I'm sorry to say his pee smelled much stronger than my paltry glandular secretion. Moppett must feed him something truly awful like human bones. My whiskers shivered at his insolence. "Once and for all. That tree is mine."

"Fat chance, fattie."

"That's it," I said, holding up my paws, claws extended. "Let's take this outside."

He grinned. "We are outside, poop."

"I know that. I mean, let's settle this like gentlecats."

Brutus chuckled. "Look, I don't mean to be rude or anything, but I eat pudgy wimps like you for breakfast. No offense." And he walked away, chortling freely.

I don't know what's worse, being pounded to a pulp by a big, beefy Persian, or having a big, beefy Persian deem you unworthy of the time and trouble to pound you to a pulp. I sighed as I watched him waddle off and disappear into the shrubbery, no doubt with a view of attaching his own additions to the Brookridge Park murder tale. By the time the night was through, I had no doubt the story going around the Brookridge rooftops and alleyways would be that a dozen vicious vampires had swooped down and viciously attacked a dozen innocent virgins with the intent of feasting on their blood and decorating the park's rustic benches and quaint old bridges with their entrails.

When I finally arrived home a couple of minutes later, I was so happy to see Zack, that I actually jumped up and licked his hands. The big guy was so touched, he cooked up some chicken liver he'd bought, and presented me the gourmet meal on a platter. I sighed a happy sigh. Now, this was the life. This was the highlight of my day. Well, this and chasing birds in the park, of course. And catching flies after dark. And cuddling on my soft blanket next to Zack when he's watching one of his silly action flicks. And... Oh, well, I'll admit it. I'm one lucky cat.

Unfortunately, the night was still young and at that moment I had no inkling of events yet to unfold. For the Brookridge Park horror had only just begun.

5

BLUEBELL

$\mathcal{Z}$ ack Zapp is a beefy fellow, built according to the blueprints laid out by the person or persons responsible for the first armored vehicle, aka, the tank. Tank was also the nickname some not-too-original schoolmate assigned to Zack at one time, and though he's the gentlest soul imaginable and wouldn't hurt a fly if it bit him on the ass, he went through high school carrying this dubious moniker, and carried it with a certain pride.

For Zack is not the brightest bulb in the bulb shop and though, as I've expressed earlier, I'm extremely fond of the big guy, there's no denying the fact that my cat brain, though probably ten times smaller in size than his, fires on more cylinders than his oversized pumpkin.

To give you an instance, I had just finished my chopped chicken liver and was licking my lips as an afterthought, when the doorbell rang and Terrell McCrady, a young artist living two doors down, stood on the porch, requesting speech.

We hadn't seen Terrell for a bit, due to the fact that he'd been out of town—staying at some posh hotel in the big city of Brussels—and Zack welcomed him with open arms, fond as he's always been of the shaggy-looking goofball.

Terrell, who's the son of Brookridge's mayor, Solomon McCrady, said he could only stay for a bit. "I'm doing the round of the neighborhood," he said as he stepped into the hallway. He had a silly smile on his face that spoke of the pleasant mood he was in. "I've got great news, Zack."

"That's great," said Zack rather lamely.

"I'm getting married."

Zack frowned. "Are you sure?"

Terrell seemed taken aback. Often, when one announces a wedding the response one expects is a little more… encouraging. "Sure I'm sure. Why, did Lexie tell you otherwise?" All of a sudden he seemed less sure of himself.

"Who," said Zack, "is Lexie?"

"Lexie Moonstone," said Terrell. "My fiancée."

"Oh, that's all right, then," said Zack.

"What's all right?"

"You didn't hear it from me, but the body of a woman was found in the park just now. I thought perhaps she was your fiancée. In which case I would imagine the wedding was off. Hard to marry a dead person, if you know what I mean." He gave Terrell the pleasant smile of one who is relieved the wedding bells will ring out after all. And I deduced from his demeanor that he'd come to the conclusion that when neighbors go to all the trouble of making house calls announcing weddings, there most probably is free food and drink on the horizon.

"What!" exclaimed Terrell, rightly perturbed.

Zack nodded. "Yep. Stabbed to death and left floating in the pond. Such a shame."

I wasn't sure if he meant the dead woman or the pond. Zack is awfully fond of feeding the ducks in the park and when dead women start floating in ponds, ducks more often than not flee the scene of the crime.

"Oh, no!"

"Oh, yes," corrected Zack the other's statement. "And the odd thing is: she was wearing some sort of a wedding dress, as if she was on her way to a wedding, possibly her own. Luckily for you, her name isn't Lexie or even Moonstone. Say, haven't I seen that girl of yours around here?"

"What was her name?" said Terrell, ignoring the question.

"Why, Lexie Moonstone of course. You just told me so yourself," said Zack, confused.

"Not my fiancée, the murder victim," said Terrell, anxious. And I could see why he would be. Even though the dead woman wasn't his Lexie, as a long-standing Brookridge citizen, it might be someone else he knew.

"Oh." Zack's brow furrowed as he attempted to recall this tidbit of information. "Um, I think Milton said her name was Zoe something. Zoe Huckleberry, I think he said. He heard it from Barbara Vale, who heard it from Fisk Grackle, who heard it from Bart Ganglion. So it must be true," he concluded a little breathlessly, for a brain the size of Zack's takes a lot of energy when taxed to its limits.

Now this is usually the part of the story where the narrator—in this case yours truly—gives a brief overview of all the persons named, as there are Milton, Barbara Vale, Fisk Grackle and Bart Ganglion. Unfortunately, adding footnotes to spine-chilling thrillers such as this story is turning out to be, is simply not done.

The reader, already on the edge of his seat and frantically biting his nails, would bludgeon the narrator with a blunt object if he were to suspend his blood-curdling tale to do so. Suffice it to say Milton Burdass-Nuttall is Zack's best friend and cohort. Barbara Vale works in City Hall as a secretary for Fisk Grackle—and is Dana's human by the way. Fisk

Grackle is assistant to the mayor. And Bart Ganglion is the local copper. The real copper, if you catch my drift, as opposed to Frank the Poodle, who only likes to think he is. Frank, by the way, is Ganglion's dog, so perhaps that's where the fluffy one gets his delusions of grandeur.

"Zoe Huckleberry," repeated Terrell thoughtfully. "Don't think I know her."

"Me, neither," said Zack. "But I do know your little squeeze, McCrady. Isn't she the redhead photographer?"

Terrell frowned unhappily. "Do you have to call her my little squeeze?"

"I'd call her your wife but since you said yourself you aren't married yet..."

"Myes, I see your point," said Terrell, and deftly changed the subject. "Well, I hope they catch whoever did it."

"Oh, I'm sure they won't," said Zack. "You know what a bungler Bart Ganglion is."

"Bart's all right once you get to know him," said Terrell. "Granted, he's no Lt. Columbo, but he's dedicated and tenacious."

"I'll say," said Zack, who had on more than one occasion been on the receiving end of Ganglion's tenaciousness.

The conversation went on for a while longer but my couch blanket was beckoning me so I returned to the living room to take a well-deserved nap before heading out once again into the night. I was closely familiar with the Terrell and Lexie story, for I had been something of the catalyst that had brought them together in the first place. Not to put too fine a point on it, I was actually present when they first met, what with me sitting in Terrell's tree trying to induce that affable young man to save me, and Lexie just happened to pass by, looking for some typical Brookridge scene for a photo shoot. To make a long story short, Terrell managed to fall, from the roof and in love with Lexie, his administering nurse, and I, after a lot of dillydallying, had finally been saved.

It was some time before Zack returned indoors, and I could see from his manner that Terrell's story had tugged at his heartstrings. Zack's heart is of a romantic nature, and the McCrady-Moonstone romance inevitably had stirred the depths of his soul. I, for one, dread the day Zack hoists Mrs. Zack over the threshold, for he and I pretty much lead the perfect bachelor life. Late-night action movies? Check. Pizza and pie at all hours of the day or night? Check. Dishes piling up in the sink? Check. Garbage bags collecting in the back garden? Check. These last two items are of particular interest to me, for dirty dishes and garbage attracts mice, and a home without mice is a boring home for any feline worth his or her salt.

For some moments, Zack sat on the couch next to me with a goofy smile on his face and staring before him with non-seeing eyes. Finally he returned to the world of the conscious and murmured a single word.

"Bluebell."

I gazed up at him with sleepy eyes awaiting further developments, but this seemed as far as his eloquence would go, and as I drifted back to sleep, I didn't give the matter further thought.

It must have been well past midnight when I awoke. Zack had gone to bed and I was alone in the living room. Stretching, I became aware of a pair of eyes staring intently in my direction from the sliding patio doors. Squinting, I recognized them as Dana's, and in them I read an urgent desire to have speech with me.

6

THE FSA REARS ITS UGLY HEAD

*a*mbling over to the kitchen, I slipped out through the pet door and onto the small patio. Dana was sitting on the wooden bench Zack had once placed there for purposes of smoking a gasper—since then he's quit smoking but the bench has remained and is now one my favorite haunts.

"What's up?" I said in my most casual voice. I don't entertain female visitors as a rule and the fact that this Siamese had come all the way down for a visit affected me strangely. I guess that's me in a nutshell: the strong yet surprisingly diffident male.

"They've found the body," she said, and didn't even have to explain which body she was talking about. I understood straightaway.

"I know," I said. "Floating in the pond, right?"

"Right." She shivered visibly. "Gruesome, isn't it?"

I reflected. "Yes, but also poetic in a way."

She gave me an odd look. "How can murder be poetic?"

"I don't know. There's just something about being gently laid to rest in a watery grave, swans gliding gracefully across the surface, water lilies gently floating by, dragonflies writing your name across the sky one last time…" I paused, for I could see that I'd failed to grip the attention of my audience of one. "What is it?"

She leaned in and whispered, "Don't look now but I think we're being watched."

The suave and astute secret agent would now, of course, casually glance over his shoulder, carelessly flicking a speck of dust off his tail, and spot the intruder in a single glance. But since I'm neither suave nor astute I simply jerked my head around and hissed, "Where? Where is he?"

"Oh, my God," said Dana, annoyed. "You really have a lot to learn, haven't you? I was just testing you, you silly tabby."

I was disappointed and failed to hide it. "So, there's no one there? You were just joshing me?"

"I was not, as you put it, joshing you, Tom. As I said, I was testing you. There's a difference."

This puzzled me. Testing me? What for? And I said as much.

She smiled, and for the first time I noticed something different about Dana. I had always thought her gorgeous as far as physical appearance goes, but her incessant flow of conversation tended to spoil whatever attraction I'd ever felt towards her. Hers was, in other words, not a butt I would ever have volunteered to sniff. But now, all of a sudden, it seemed as if she had dropped the charade of the rather vapid, addle-brained bombshell and was looking at me with the gleam of keen intelligence in her lovely amber eyes.

"There's something we've been meaning to tell you for a long time, Tom, but we didn't feel you were quite ready yet. Now, though, we think you are."

"We? Who's we?"

She cleared her throat and swelled a bit, as one will when on the verge of imparting some truly important information.

"No, wait," I said, smiling. "Is this about Stevie and that mouse again? Just tell him all's well as far as I'm concerned." She opened her mouth to speak but I held up a paw. "I confess I was mad at the time. And who wouldn't be? I had marked that mouse for my own when Stevie suddenly swooped in and grabbed it. Right from under my nose. Not fair, I felt. Not playing the game. But now I realize the poor fella was probably hungry. Father Sam must be stinting on kibble, I guess. So tell him all is forgiven and forgotten. Clean slate. How's that?"

I must confess I was feeling pretty good about myself. I'm not much of a Christian cat, but all that jazz about turning the other whisker suddenly sounded very plausible to me. Then something Dana said made me realize that once again I'd failed to grip my audience's attention.

"Can you put a sock in it for just one minute?" she said. "This isn't about Stevie and it most certainly isn't about some mouse he allegedly swiped."

"He did swipe it," I mumbled. "Nothing alleged about it."

"That's fine. Now will you listen?"

I said I would, and even this seemed to irk her so I made a gesture of locking my lips and throwing away the key.

She shook her head. "I don't know whether this is such a good idea after all," she said. "And if it was up to me..."

"If what was up to you?" I said, having forgotten my promise to shut it.

She ignored me, and went on. "But since it isn't..." She seemed to steel herself and turned those amber eyes on me. I don't mind telling you it disconcerted me somewhat. You don't see all that many Persian cats with amber eyes, blue being more in fashion with the breed. "Have you ever heard about the FSA?"

7

REMARKABLE REVELATIONS

I assured her I hadn't heard of the FSA, and added that if this was some hot new brand of cat food, she could sign me up immediately. I'm always up for testing new cat food. "I'm your man," I said in conclusion, after giving her my candid opinion on Whiskas, Hill's, Felix, Friskies, Go Cat, Purina, Gourmet and Sheba. A scorching look from my companion made me cut short my lecture on the pros and cons of cat food, though.

"FSA stands for the Feline Security Agency, an espionage agency run by cats and dealing particularly with matters of—"

"You're a spy?" I said, surprised and excited.

"Yes, I'm a spy," she said. "Now if you will let me finish…"

"You mean like James Bond and stuff? Top-secret missions and highly classified information and security clearance and shifty-eyed villainous psychopathic madmen and—"

"Yes, yes, yes!" she said, annoyed. "God! I don't know anyone like you for talking."

I considered this a compliment and I said so, though I had the distinct impression that's not the way she'd intended it.

"Now the FSA is not an ordinary intelligence agency," she went on.

"No shit," I said. "It's run by cats."

"Exactly. We're the first and only intelligence agency run by animals, and we pride ourselves on the fact. But what makes us really special is that we are not engaged in some intelligence war with other spy agencies, like our human counterparts are."

"I know what you mean," I said. "The Russians are spying on the Americans are spying on the Chinese are spying on the Russians…"

"And it goes on and on. We are not like that. We don't spy on other feline agencies because there are no other feline agencies to spy on."

"Perhaps there's a canine agency?" I ventured, for I'd just seen a movie called 'Cats and Dogs' the other day with Zack, and the set-up had struck me as sound.

"No. There's no canine agency; and if there was, and I'm not aware of the existence of one, we wouldn't consider it our enemy anyway. In fact dogs are an integral part of our organization and help us out on a regular basis."

"Frank?" I said.

She nodded. "He knows and he's one of our many informants. Now, you'll probably wonder what our main purpose is?"

"I do," I said eagerly, and I did. I'd never heard about this FSA and wondered how they'd been able to keep it a secret from one as inquisitive as I am.

"Have you ever heard of the concept of the Guardian Angel?"

I had to laugh at this. "Those chubby-looking dudes

wearing diapers and hovering around on their wings of fairy dust?"

She grimaced. "Not exactly. Though that's probably the way humans like to imagine their guardian angels to be. It would be closer to the truth to say that a guardian angel is a furry mammal with a longish tail, short snout and retractile claws." She paused and I blinked.

"Oh," I said, trying to imagine an angel with a tail, snort snout and claws and covered in fur. "But they still have golden curls, chubby cheeks and wings, right?"

She laughed for the first time and I was relieved. "No, silly. The real guardian angels are us, cats. We are the ones tasked with the responsibility of looking after humans any way we can. Well, at least card-carrying members of the FSA, of course," she added as she saw my look of incredulity.

"We are supposed to look after humans?" I said, and my mind boggled at the notion. "But I thought it was the other way around. Zack looks after me. I don't look after him."

"Now, that's where you're wrong," she said gently, for she could see I was wrestling with the concept. "How many times have you saved Zack from harm?"

"Zero times," I said truthfully. "Generally I do my thing and he does his thing and the twain only meet at night when we share the couch to watch silly action movies and other such nonsense."

"That's where you're mistaken," said Dana. "Do you remember about one month ago when Zack had left the gas stove burning even after he'd removed the pan? The house could have gone up in flames if he hadn't switched off the burner."

I did remember the incident. My keen sense of smell had detected the omission even before the towel had been set aflame. And though I'd given a squeak of surprise at the time, I didn't remember having done anything to prevent the disaster from taking place. After all, I'm not a dog. I don't go in for that sort of thing. Then a thought struck me. "How do you know about that?"

"Ah, that's where the plot thickens," she spoke mysteriously. "Now, did the house burn down that day?"

I reflected. "No, it didn't," I admitted. "Zack noticed in time, hurried over to the kitchen and put out the fire. And good thing he did. He'd just bought a 15 kilo supply of fresh kibble and that would have been toast if he hadn't."

"Yes, well, you may wonder why he suddenly noticed?"

I twitched my ears. "To tell you the truth…"

"No, I didn't think so."

There was a hint of reproof in her voice, but I let it go. "So how did you know?"

She leaned in and said in a low voice, her eyes twinkling, "Because I was there."

"Hah!" I said, more in surprise than disbelief. "Huh?"

"I was there from the moment you sent out the signal."

"What signal? I didn't send out any signal."

"You did. The moment you sensed the danger, you automatically emitted a signal, which was picked up at FSA headquarters, which dispatched me to the Zapp homestead. I then nudged Zack into action, with the result that you know."

I scratched my scalp with one claw. This didn't make any sense. "But how come I didn't see you?" was only the first of many questions that came to mind.

"That's because I was invisible."

8

BRUTUS REVISITED

"Oh, boy," I said. This was really getting beyond me. The spy story she'd dished up was fine, and so was the FSA. But this stuff about guardian angels and invisible cats... I realized Dana was either mad as a hatter or simply pulling my leg.

I looked up and noticed a full moon was out tonight, and suddenly I felt a strong yearning for my favorite tree. There'd probably be field mice in the park, and perhaps even a small rat or two. An empty feeling in the pit of my stomach reminded me there were more important things to do than listen to the ramblings of a certified nutcase. "I think I'm off," I said therefore.

Dana stiffened. "Is that so?"

"Yah. The weather is fine and the vast wilderness awaits the lone hunter."

"Don't you want to hear the rest of the story?"

"Nah, think I'll skip this one. Invisible cats, guardian angels, strange messages... I'm not so much into fantasy tales myself. I'm more of an action thriller guy. See ya."

And before she could feed me any more of her patent

nonsense, I'd taken a quick leap from the bench and was off running at a speed I knew she would have a hard time matching. Unless she took wings and flew, of course. I grinned at the prospect. Mad as a coot, that dame.

It seemed there wasn't much substance to Dana's story, though, for I reached the park without any angels crossing my path, and was up in my tree enjoying the view spread out before me without so much as one invisible cat breathing a word of protest. I sighed a long sigh of relief at finally being on my own again. Who did Dana think she was fooling? Hah. Not me.

I looked down at the peaceful scene below. The notion that a murder had taken place there gave me a tiny shiver of apprehension, but it soon passed. I'd spent so many happy hours in the company of this tree that horrific events like the one I'd been a witness to were blotted out by the thousands of good memories afforded me.

I stretched out languidly on the thick branch that was home away from home and closed my eyes to slits for a moment, quietly observing the wonders of the night. Other cats were on the prowl, but they all knew better than to disturb me. I'd marked this tree for my own and apart from Dana, no one ever bothered me here. Then I heard Brutus speaking irreverently to some poor schmuck and I was reminded that there was one other cat that habitually trespassed on my private property.

"Hey, fathead!"

I wondered who the poor cat was that the big brute had selected for a game of browbeating this time. Probably some feckless youth wandering out into the park for the first time in his life.

"I'm talking to you, meatball."

So sad, I thought, that bullies have to pick on smaller cats just to boost their own self-esteem. There probably was some psychological explanation for this kind of behavior, and I was pretty sure it had something to do with the length of the thug's tail, which was surprisingly short.

"Hey, Tommy!"

I opened my eyes with a start. Not only did it now occur to me that Brutus was addressing me and not some random stranger, but all of a sudden his voice sounded a lot closer than before. I looked up and lo and behold: my nemesis had parked his big butt on the same branch I habitually selected for my nighttime entertainment, and now sat staring at me with that mocking expression on his ugly visage.

"Look, Brutus. If I've told you once, I've told you a million times," I began, but he didn't let me finish.

"Zip it, hairball. I'm not here to pick a fight with you."

"Oh? Well, you could have fooled me," I retorted with some hauteur.

"It's about that dame," he said with something approaching embarrassment in his voice.

"Dame? I don't know what you're talking about," I said.

He scuffed his paw on the branch and chipped off a piece of bark in the process. "The dead dame. The floater. You remember."

"Oh, that dame."

"Yeah, that dame. I've seen her."

This struck me as odd. "Seen her? Where?"

"In my dreams," came the intriguing reply.

"In your dreams," I said skeptically.

"Yes, I've seen her in my dreams," he said. "And what I was wondering…" His voice trailed off and he seemed to swallow something jagged lodged in his throat. Probably his pride.

"Yes?" I was still fogged to a degree. This was turning out to be quite the night for oddball confessions.

"Well, you saw what happened. Have you been having bad dreams? Napmares?"

I laughed what I hoped was a mocking laugh. "No, my dear Brutus. I don't dream about the incident. In fact I'd all but forgotten about the whole thing until you showed up and dredged it up from the dead past where I left it."

"Oh," he said, and chipped some more bark from my branch. "Well, I keep seeing some waterlogged human corpse trying to attract my attention every time I close my eyes. It's not much fun, I can tell you."

"Yes, I can see how that would be annoying."

"She seems to want something, but for the life of me, I can't figure out what it is. Every time I offer her a piece of my codfish, she sighs and vanishes."

"What I'd suggest is that you have a long talk with Dana. You know Dana, don't you? Yes, of course you do. Now, you don't have to take my word for it, but you and she have a lot in common."

"You think so?" he said. And he gave me a look of such hopefulness my heart almost bled for the brute. But then I was strong again.

"Yes, I do." I would have added they were both potty and would therefore get along like only two inmates of the loony bin can, but refrained from doing so. One has to remain civil on these occasions.

He looked at me kind of strangely, and finally muttered something that I can only describe as broken words of gratitude, and pottered off.

"Phew," I said, as soon as he was out of sight, and laid down my weary head for a much needed rest. But, still my troubles were not over.

"You shouldn't have done that," a voice spoke from the darkness, and, looking up to see with whom I had the pleasure, I saw that… there was no one there.

9

GHOSTS IN THE PARK

*N*ow, I don't know what your policy is on disembodied voices suddenly coming out of nowhere and intruding upon what is supposed to be a perfectly wonderful evening, but I have to admit to not liking them. And I said as much. In fact the exact words I used were, "Could you please leave me alone and harass someone else?"

"No, I cannot," the disembodied voice retorted, and with not a little bit of pique I might add.

I groaned both in spirit and in body.

"You could have prevented what happened, little one," said the voice, "but you didn't. You had it in your power to stop me from being murdered and you didn't."

Now, you would probably have expected me to pick up on the M word but I had stopped listening when the voice mentioned something about me being little. It perked me up a great deal. All my life people have called me freakishly large, and here was some unknown voice coming from up above calling me little. So you can't blame me for jumping to conclusions.

"Thank you, God," I said. "I've always said I wasn't big. And thank you for finally answering my prayers. I've been praying for a long time, even though I wasn't even sure you existed. I'm so glad that you do and that you've taken time out of your busy—"

"I'm not God," thundered the voice. And now I noticed it sounded kinda hollow, as if it came from a tomb or something.

"Oh," I said, a little taken aback. And then enlightenment struck. I cocked an eye at the upper branches of the tree where the voice seemed to be coming from. "Guardian angel?" I said, remembering something Dana had said.

An unearthly sigh drifted down and the voice spoke again. "I am not your guardian angel, little one. I'm the soul of the woman you allowed to be murdered."

This rattled me somewhat, but nevertheless I trudged on. "Well, allowed is a big word," I sputtered. If this person wasn't God or my guardian angel, there was only one other option: Brutus or one of his gang was playing a practical joke on me. I now saw all. It had struck me as odd that Brutus, notoriously the toughest cat on the block, would suddenly go all wimpy on me but now his behavior made perfect sense: he was simply setting me up for the arrival of this 'ghost'.

I gave a knowing smile. "The game is up, my friend. The cat's out of the bag. I know what you're up to. So you'd better come on down or else I'm coming up there. And you don't want that, I assure you."

A sad rattle sounded from higher up the tree. "It is true. It's not what I want for you."

"You're damn skippy it's not what you want. So, you better scoot and tell Brutus his psychological game didn't work out as planned."

"You are right," heaved the voice mournfully. "It is certainly not how I planned this evening to go."

"You have to tell me how you're doing that thing with the voice," I said. "It's a great trick for Halloween."

"Alas, I won't be here when Halloween comes around." The voice—I still hadn't figured out to whom it belonged—seemed to be drifting farther and farther away somehow, growing weaker if you will. "Next time, little one, pay more attention and act when called upon. Don't be afraid to intervene…"

And with these words, the voice died away and silence once again reigned. Well, as far as silence can reign in a small town park in the middle of the night. "Hello," I said tentatively. "Are you there?"

But nothing stirred. And though of course I knew I was the victim of some kind of practical joke, I still felt strangely dejected. The voice had sounded so… sad. And, frankly, that just doesn't fit the MO of Brutus or his amigos. It takes some measure of intelligence to be sad, is what I mean to say. And those guys just don't have it. Inane giggling is what I would have expected. Not this otherworldly melancholy.

I shivered in spite of the balmy spring weather and wondered when the next surprise would mar my peaceful existence. Well, as it was, I didn't have long to wait, for I'd just picked up on some promising squeaking sounding from down below that almost certainly was mouse-like in origin, when yet another voice addressed me.

"Well? Do you believe me now?"

As I might have guessed, it was Dana, back to badger me with her nonsense. I searched around to tell her what was what, when I noticed to my surprise there was no one there. And yet her voice had come from somewhere in my rear. Very close by it had sounded. Right about where the tip of my tail now raked the air in search of feline life forms and finding none.

"Can't see me, can you?" Dana said. And I could have

NIC SAINT

sworn she was sitting right next to me. Once again my tail swooshed through the air and found nothing to arrest its sweep.

"Dana?" I said, slightly spooked now. "Is that you?"

"Of course it's me... little one."

I started. Little one. That's how that spooky friend of Brutus had called me. But how would Dana know about that? Had she been spying on me?

"You... you heard that?"

"Of course I did. I was sitting here the whole time."

I wheeled round. Still no sign of Dana. "You were... here?" I was starting to get really rattled now. How was she doing this? Camouflage?

"Sure. Haven't you noticed? Oh, but I forgot. You don't believe I can turn myself invisible, do you?"

I laughed but, though I intended to make it sound nonchalant and carefree, even to my own ears it sounded shrill and terrified. "That's a good one, Dana. Good joke."

"It's not a joke, Tom. I am invisible."

"But that's impossible."

"It's possible. And that voice you heard? It belonged to the woman we saw killed earlier tonight."

I have to confess I shivered from eyebrows to paw pads at these words. "That was... a ghost?"

"Yep. You should feel honored. Those were that poor woman's very last words here on earth before her spirit joined the afterlife."

"A dead woman's ghost..." I swallowed heavily. "spoke to me?"

"Quite an experience, don't you think?"

"Quite," I said, and had to lie down for a bit, suddenly feeling faint.

"So now do you believe me?"

I moaned. "Come on, Dana. This is no way to treat a guy.

38

Drop the camouflage act and show yourself, will you? This isn't funny."

There was a momentary silence, then all of a sudden the air in front of me seemed to shimmer slightly, then a bright light flashed that almost blinded me, and the next moment Dana was sitting next to me, licking her paws as if nothing happened.

10

THE PLOT THICKENS

I gasped at the sight of her. "How did you do that?" I cried.

She studied her paw. "I told you. I can make myself invisible."

"But that's impossible!"

"You keep repeating that. Didn't you see me with your own eyes? Or rather, didn't see me?"

I had to admit that I had, though I could hardly believe it. "But, but, but…" I sputtered.

"Yes?" she said sweetly, looking at me from under her long lashes.

"But, but, but…" I tried once more.

"If I didn't know you better, I would think that you're suffering from speechlessness. But no, that's impossible. Tommy the cat is never lost for words."

"I, I, I…"

She groaned. "Look, the explanation is perfectly simple, and if you had listened to me instead of running off like that —extremely rude of you, by the way—you would have been prepared when Zoe Huckleberry came to bid you farewell and would have had something better to say to her than some nonsense about Halloween or guardian angels. God knows she only had a few moments left here on this mortal coil." She shook her head. "What a waste to spend them talking to you."

I still wasn't completely recuperated from seeing Dana explode onto the scene like that, but I was aware that this was some sort of verbal abuse she was slinging my way. "For your information, we had a perfectly interesting conversation. And Zoe, if that's her name, had some very nice things to say about me."

"Like what?" said Dana.

"Like…" Here she rather had me. What had this Zoe ghost been saying to me? Then I remembered something rather neat. "Like the fact that she complimented me on my slim form," I said triumphantly.

"She did not," scoffed Dana.

"She did too. She kept calling me little one and—"

"You seem to forget I heard the entire conversation."

"Oh," I said. I had indeed forgotten this one small detail. Then something else occurred to me. "Say, if you were here, why didn't you talk to her yourself?"

"I…" Now it was Dana's turn to be speechless. She pursed her lips. "I didn't want to interfere."

I laughed. "Now that's the lamest excuse for not talking to a ghost I've ever heard." And that was the weirdest sentence I'd ever formulated. Talking to a ghost? Was this for real?

"I know," she said, and stared up at the moon for a bit, chewing her lower lip. "I probably should have said something, shouldn't I? I just didn't think she'd be out of here so soon. I thought we'd have more time."

"She did leave quite abruptly," I said. And it was true. One moment she was here and the next she was gone with the wind. Or whatever it is these ghosts travel on when passing beyond the veil, if veils are what they pass beyond.

"I hope you realize now how important our work is," Dana said, her mind having returned from the beyond to the present.

Actually, I hadn't realized much, apart from the fact that ghosts seemed to enjoy my company all of a sudden, and that Dana had mastered some neat party trick creating the illusion she was invisible, but the girl seemed undone by the recent meeting with the dearly departed, so I bit my tongue and kept quiet.

"The FSA doesn't proselytize, you know," she continued, as I had expected she would. "Based on certain criteria, it very carefully selects its candidates and then enlists them. Tonight was your first test and I'm sorry to say that you failed."

"I failed? How?" Even though I didn't buy into Dana's fantasy stories, I still felt rightfully offended.

"Like Zoe said; you had the chance to save her and you didn't."

I rolled my eyes at this one. "Well, if someone had told me what I was supposed to do, perhaps I would have done it, don't you think?"

"That's just the point: every single candidate enlisted before instinctively did the right thing even without anyone telling him, or her, what to do. You're the first one to let the woman die."

"Women have died before?" I said, confused.

Dana nodded emphatically. "Sure. Standard operating procedure. We stage a scene to see how the candidate will react and then monitor response time, physiological and psychological markers, emotional stress parameters, the works."

"But that's awful!" I said. "You're murdering human

beings just to see how some cat will respond? I find that just about the lowest thing I've ever heard. That's just... horrible!"

Dana didn't respond but merely beamed at me.

"I don't think it's funny," I said, indignant.

Dana put a paw on my shoulder but I shrugged it off. "See, I knew you were going to say that," she said, and grinned. "And that's why you weren't kicked out of the program. Even though you're probably the weirdest candidate we've ever had, there's something so... human... about you that simply begs for induction into the FSA."

"I don't want to be inducted into your rotten FSA," I said with some vehemence. "I may not like all humans quite as much as I like Zack, but that doesn't mean I condone sacrificing them for the purpose of that murderous club of yours! I think it's disgusting, immoral, beyond contempt, and I plan to have a serious talk to whoever is in charge of this FSA. And I'll have you know, I intend to stop this abomination and stop it now."

To my surprise she let out a ringing guffaw at these brave words, possibly the bravest ones I've ever spoken. I was more than a little disconcerted.

"Bravo," she said, as she clapped her paws, something I'd never seen any cat do before. "I think it's time now to tell you all."

"All?" I cried. "There's more?"

"Oh, yes. A lot more."

11

A NEW PARTNER FOR AGENT TOM

"*W*hat more can there be?" I wailed. "Blood sacrifices under the light of the full moon? Gorging on human flesh? What?"

"First of all, we owe you an apology."

"I'd say you do."

"Because there never was a murder. No one died tonight."

"Of course someone died," I said. "Zoe Huckleberry. She came to say goodbye just now. You heard her."

"Zoe Huckleberry doesn't exist. She's just a character in a play. And so is Jack Mackintosh."

"Jack who?"

"The guy with the knife."

"I don't understand," I said. She had completely lost me now.

"It's like this. Every year in the springtime we select new candidates for the FSA. And one of the tests is what we like to call the murder scene. Now each year in springtime, the Brookridge Theatrical Society likes to perform an Agatha Christie type play—"

"The Mousetrap!" I said, for I'd heard about it being

performed the previous year. Zack had almost secured a part for himself in it and I'd hoped he'd get it and bring home the mouse. Unfortunately, Fisk Grackle, the mayor's secretary, had been selected to play Zack's part. Clear case of nepotism, Zack had said, for the mayor was chairman of the Theatrical Society.

"This year it's Murder in the Park. They like to stage a different one each year. But that's fine. Whatever the play, there's bound to be a murder scene that needs to be rehearsed before opening night."

"Of course." I was starting to see what she was driving at.

"And when the weather is fine, the actors like to come to the park for their rehearsals."

"Oh…" I said, for I now saw all. Again. "You mean…"

She nodded slowly. "Yes, that scene we witnessed together was part of the play."

"But I saw…" I furrowed my red fluffy brow, for what had I actually seen? A man brandishing a knife, and when I next looked down, a woman was lying there, struck down. Or so it seemed. "I never saw the actual murder," I said slowly.

"Go on," said Dana, encouragingly.

"But what about the body floating in the pond? They couldn't stage that, could they?"

"Did you see the body?"

"Brutus!" I said. "Brutus told me." I eyed Dana with a measure of apprehension. "Don't tell me Brutus is part of the FSA."

"He isn't," Dana reassured me. "But as I started to tell you when you ran out on me before, we have the power to plant certain suggestions into people's heads, and also other animals. That's how Zack suddenly noticed the gas burner was still on, and that's how Brutus thought he'd heard the story about the body in the pond and what made him so anxious to tell you all about it. Oh, and the voice of Zoe

Huckleberry you heard just now?" She tapped her chest in a gesture of pride. "*Moi.*"

"But why?" I said. "Why the whole charade? Why go to all that trouble?"

"Because of you, Agent Tom." Now it was my chest Dana tapped, or should I say punched, for she was surprisingly muscular for her size and build. Probably all lean muscle.

"Because of me?"

"All part of the test. What we want to establish first and foremost, is empathy. Does the candidate feel empathetic enough towards humans that he'd be willing to put his life on the line to save them? Well, since you more or less failed the first part of the test, we wanted to give you a second chance by introducing Zoe's 'ghost' and see if she couldn't get a little remorse out of you. You know, a little penitence. Unfortunately you failed us again."

"Well, how was I to know she was for real?" I said defensively.

"I know," she said. "We had unfortunately overestimated your, um, judgment somewhat. And I was just about to give up on you when all of a sudden you blew your top. And showed more empathy towards human beings than any candidate I've ever interviewed."

"Well, it just isn't right," I said, all the old pique returning. "You can't go around murdering humans."

"Well, once again, for the record: we don't. You understand that now, don't you?"

"Sure," I said, though I couldn't suppress a twinge of doubt. First Zoe Huckleberry was murdered, then she wasn't, and then she didn't even exist. All very confusing, if you see what I mean.

"Good. The FSA mission statement clearly stipulates as its number one priority the saving of human lives. We do this consistently. We do this globally. And we've been doing this ever since the first human started walking on his hind legs."

"Silly habit, that," I said. Why walk on two legs when you can walk on four, I meant to say.

"So, what about it?"

I blinked. Was this another test? "What about what?"

"Are you in?"

"Oh, sure," I said, though I had no idea what she was talking about. "In what exactly?"

"The FSA, of course. Do you accept it as your life's mission to serve and protect human beings? To spy out their lives and see to it that no harm comes to them? In other words, do you feel up to it, Agent Tom?"

At these words I perked up considerably. Agent Tom. I had to admit it had a nice ring to it. Partnered with Agent Dana, Agent Tom embarks on the boldest missions, carries out the most exciting assignments, launches the most taxing operations and saves human lives left, right and center. Sure I felt up to it. Who wouldn't? I thrust out my paw. "Agent Tom reporting for duty, Agent Dana."

Dana tapped my paw and shook it once, vigorously. Quite brawny.

"It will be my pleasure to serve the human race," I said, trying to strike the right note. Bold, yet sophisticated. Suave, yet humble. And always, of course, debonair. In other words, from now on my name was Tom. Agent Tom.

"Wonderful," Dana said appreciatively, and it amazed me how different she seemed now from the rather vapid Dana I'd always known. Fantastic acting skills, no doubt about it. How much I could learn from her. Of course, being partners, I'd simply assimilate all of those skills through osmosis.

"So what happens now?" I said, all of a sudden quite anxious to start on the road to feline espionage.

"Now you meet your partner and start your training," said Dana simply.

"Great!" I said, and suddenly perceived our duo had turned into a trio. A big, white-haired Raggamuffin with reddish whiskers came waddling towards us, precariously teetering on the branch and looking very uncomfortable as he kept darting glances at the ground below.

"Stevie!" I cried, for I had instantly recognized that notorious mouse thief. "What are you doing here?"

"Why do you guys always have to climb trees?" he complained. "Why can't you just stay with your four paws on the ground like normal cats?"

"Normal cats like climbing trees, Stevie," said Dana, giving him a sniff.

"Look, Stevie," I said, liking none of this sniffing business, "we're in the middle of a very important meeting here. So buzz off, will you?"

"Buzz off?" he whined, now hugging the branch with all claws extended and pressing his head flat against the bark. "But I just got here."

"And now you're going again," I pointed out.

"Not a chance. I'm not turning back if my life depended on it. The only way I'm getting out of this tree is firmly in the grip of some burly, highly capable fireman. So, Dana, just tell me why you asked me to meet you here and then I'll start mewling for the cavalry, all right? Do you think those guys work nights? But of course they do. Fires don't keep regular hours, do they? Ha, ha. How silly of me."

I was appalled. "Asked him?" I said incredulously. "You asked him?"

Dana gave me a curt nod. "Agent Tom, meet Agent Stevie. He will be your partner."

"My what?" I cried.

Stevie glanced up at me apologetically. "Don't look at me,

buddy. It wasn't my idea. I told her you wouldn't like it, but she wouldn't listen. Still sore about that mouse I pinched, are you? Boy, you certainly know how to hold a grudge. Let bygones be bygones, is what I always say. Say, what do you like best? Agent Stevie or Agent Steve? Personally I think I'll go with Steve. Sounds more butch, doesn't it? Like a real spy?"

I merely heaved a hollow groan in response. Little did I know that right then and there, one of the great partnerships in feline history had begun. All I could think was that I had just gotten myself into another nice mess. And Dana? She merely smiled.

LUCY KNICX RETURNS

I was still sitting on the same tree branch with Dana and Stevie, slowly coming to grips with this new reality facing me, when a thought struck me.

"Won't the whole town of Brookridge now think that the actress playing Zoe Huckleberry was murdered by the actor with the pimple?"

"The whole town of Brookridge?" said Dana. "Of course not. The only ones who know about this are you and Brutus. And I made sure that the memory implant I installed in Brutus only lasted long enough to convince you about Zoe floating in the pond. By now he's forgotten all about the affair."

"But Brutus said he'd heard it from—"

Dana waved an impatient paw. "All part of the implant. He didn't hear it from anyone but invisible old me."

I frowned thoughtfully. "But what about Zack and Terrell? Won't they go blabbing the story around town?"

Dana eyed me strangely. "Zack and Terrell? They don't know about this."

"Sure they do. Zack was telling the story to Terrell. He

said he heard it from Milton who heard it from Barbara Vale who heard it from Fisk Grackle who heard it from Bart Ganglion himself. And I'm sure the story must have spread all over Brookridge by now. Your Barbara doesn't stint on gossip, you know that."

As I've mentioned before, Barbara Vale is Dana's human. She works as a secretary at City Hall and is a very, um, sociable woman.

"But that's impossible," said Dana, now looking thoroughly perturbed.

"Why impossible? Barbara works faster than the Internet, Zack always says."

Dana looked up, and there was a worried expression in her big, brown eyes. "It's impossible because I never implanted the story in any of those people."

"Then how…" I began, but all of a sudden I was interrupted by a ghoulish voice sounding from somewhere in the vicinity of the second branch from the top of my tree.

"You should have saved me, little one," groaned the voice.

Dana and I started violently. Stevie merely winced. Throughout our conversation he'd been clinging to the tree branch, and this voice clearly didn't mean as much to him as it did to us.

"You should have saved me when you had the chance," said the voice.

"Who are you?" said Dana, a slight trill in her voice. "Is this some kind of joke?"

"Hey, that was my line," I protested.

"Who is that?" said Stevie, joining in.

"Probably Brutus," I said, taking a wild guess. But from the look on Dana's face I had the distinct impression something else was going on.

"I am Lucy Knicx," said the voice, drifting in and out of earshot, like the wailing of the wind. It was all quite spooky, I can tell you. "And I was murdered tonight... I was rehearsing a scene for Murder in the Park, the play... performing with the Brookridge Theatrical Society."

"Zoe Huckleberry," I said.

"That's right," moaned Lucy. "That was my part... I was playing with... when suddenly he stuck a knife... next moment... floating in the pond... no way to treat a girl."

"So it did happen," I said.

Dana nodded distractedly. The sudden appearance of Lucy's ghost seemed to have rattled her even more than it had me. Of course, when the highest purpose of your organization is the saving of human lives and you organize a test for new recruits, it's rather disconcerting when in the course of this test a human life is lost.

"Who was playing the part of Jack Mackintosh?" said Dana.

"Rick Mascarpone was supposed to... last minute replaced by an understudy... never met him before... quite good performance, except for the finale."

"What was his name?" said Dana.

"His name was... quite good-looking and charming... until he stuck a knife in my back... bluebell..."

"His name," repeated Dana.

"... have to go now... Saint-Peter calling... hope he has plenty of rice pudding... starving," said Lucy. Then there was some sort of a popping sound, and silence returned.

13

MEET THE PETERBALDS

"*D*arn it," said Dana, stomping the tree branch. It slightly swayed under the impact.

"Hey," cried Stevie, digging his claws deeper into the cork. "Don't do that."

"Stevie," I said.

"Steve," he corrected.

"Steve," I amended, "don't you think it's kind of odd for a secret agent to be afraid of heights?"

"I'm not afraid of heights," he said. "I just don't like to climb trees."

"Will you two be quiet," said Dana, who was gazing in the direction Lucy's voice had sounded from. We were quiet for a spell, but nothing stirred. Dana sighed. "This is bad," she said. "Very, very bad."

"What's so bad about it?" I said. "We knew Zoe Huckleberry was killed."

She rolled her eyes. "That was a fake," she said. "Merely a ruse we applied as a test."

"Oh, that's right," I said. I'd forgotten about that again. "Well, you can't blame me for losing track," I said. "First she was murdered, then she wasn't, and now she was." I eyed her suspiciously. "Don't tell me this is another one of your tests."

"No, it's not," she said sharply. "What we saw was real after all. If I had only known…" She hung her head.

"Had known what?" said Stevie, having come to the conclusion he wasn't going to plummet to an untimely death after all.

I explained to him the state of affairs, and to his credit he grasped it instantly.

"Great!" he exclaimed. "That means we've got our first case, Agent Tom."

"I don't think so, Agent Stevie, um, Steve. We're trainees. Trainees don't take cases."

"Why not?" he said. "On the job training."

I had to admit it wasn't such a bad idea. "He's right," I said. "We could crack this case and learn a ton."

"No way," said Dana. "This is for professionals only. You two would only get in the way of the real spies."

"But we're here. We're eyewitnesses to what happened. I'm sure that if we put our heads together—"

"Yeah," chimed in Stevie. "Tommy and I will simply put our heads together. Like this." And he proceeded to demonstrate his point by giving me a head-butt. And in spite of all of the fluff it hurt.

"Ouch!" I said, rubbing the spot. "What did you do that for?"

"Just to demonstrate my point," said Stevie apologetically. "So we're on for the case?"

"No way," said Dana with some vehemence. "And that's my last word. In fact, I think it's best if you two head on home now. The moment the training starts, I will let you know."

"You're calling in the cavalry?" I said, and I couldn't hide my disappointment.

"I am. Now scoot."

"I'm not moving," said Stevie, to whom the prospect of leaving this tree under his own steam was tantamount to suicide. "I... like it here."

Without much further ado, Dana gave the unfortunate Ragamuffin a forceful shove and sent him plummeting down. As his big, hairy body hurtled through the air, Stevie gave a piercing scream, but finally managed to land on all fours on the mulch below.

"That's no way to treat a fellow agent," the fluffy cat muttered under his breath, as he started checking himself for injuries.

"Go home," called Dana after him. "This is a crime scene now."

"Oh, all right," mumbled Stevie, and stalked off.

"You too, Tom," said Dana. "There's nothing further you can do here."

"Oh, but I can," I said, in a last-ditch effort to change her mind. "With Stevie gone, you can speak freely now. I'm sure I can be of assistance. After all, I was here when it all happened. I saw the whole thing."

"Get lost, Tom," she said. "I've got this."

I wanted to say that so did I, but there was something in her voice that told me I better made for the exit, so I toddled off, my tail held high, and left the scene.

And as I was threading my way back home, cursing under my breath about high-minded spymasters taking over my tree, I noticed a strange procession approaching. Three Peterbald cats came trotting my way. You know the breed: Russian in origin, very skinny, no fur, and big ears. The moment I saw them I knew they were FSA, and I greeted them like long-lost brothers.

"Hi, you guys," I said warmly.

The three cats stared at me with ill-concealed hostility.

"Mind your own business," hissed the first one.

"Get lost," growled the second one.

"Beat it," grunted the third.

I had the impression they didn't like me very much. Of course I could be wrong. Perhaps I simply hadn't given them the secret handshake yet. Whatever that was.

"The crime scene is right over there," I said, helpful as ever, and I pointed a dainty claw in the direction of my elm tree.

"Scram, squirt," snarled the biggest one of the trio, and made a menacing move in my direction. He had a scar the shape of a sledgehammer above his right eye. It wasn't that he was big, exactly. Just extremely sinewy. And I was thinking I wouldn't like to meet this guy alone in the dark, when I realized I *was* meeting him alone in the dark. Him and two of his equally freakishly sinewy buddies. I shivered slightly.

"Right ho," I said. "I'll be pushing along then, shall I?"

This time they didn't speak, but merely threw menacing glances in my direction. If looks could kill… And since they didn't seem all that eager for the pleasure of my company, I gave them a merry 'cheerio' and pottered off. Not that I wasn't anxious to do so. They were definitely not the most cheery brothers. Were all FSA agents like this, I wondered? And for a moment there I even wavered in my allegiance to the cause. But then I thought of Dana, and I was strong again. At least one cat in the FSA employ was all right. Though she did steal my tree.

14

ELEMENTARY, MY DEAR STEVIE

"She kick you out as well?" The sad voice came from a bench nearby. I glanced over and saw that Stevie had sought the heights again, though this time not as high as before. I ambled over and hopped onto the bench next to him. He might be daft, but he was my partner now.

"Yeah, I guess when things get serious, the FSA has no need for rookies," I said.

"I still think we could have helped," he said.

"Well, we still can," I said, for a thought had just occurred to me.

"What do you mean?"

"We're agents in the employ of the FSA now. And our mission is to help humans, right?"

"Right."

"So?"

"So what?"

"So we don't need Dana's permission to fulfill our mission, do we?"

His jaw drooped as he mulled this over. "Um, I guess not?" he ventured.

"Of course we don't. Let's you and I solve this crime and present Dana with the solution, and our place in the FSA hallmark of fame will be guaranteed."

"Does the FSA have a hallmark of fame?" he said, a little dubiously.

"Sure it has, and we'll be in it."

"Oh." The prospect seemed to please him, for he hitched up his jaw and managed a smile. "That's fine, then."

"Better than fine. It's great."

"Great," he echoed.

"So, let's have your ideas on the matter. What do you think happened? We need to establish a timeline."

"Um," he said, closing his eyes. "What happened?" he said slowly.

"Let's start with what we know."

"Yes," he said. "What we know." He opened his eyes. "What do we know?"

"Well, we know that Lucy Knicx—"

"Funny name, that," he remarked, and snickered.

"Well, be that as it may, Lucy Knicx was rehearsing a scene for the upcoming play—"

"Did you know Sam is going to be in the play?" He nodded emphatically. "He's playing the butler. Imagine that. A priest playing a butler. Funny, that. And he's been asked to direct the thing as well."

"Funny," I said, though I failed to see the humor in the situation. "We know she was playing the role of Zoe Huckle-berry, and was supposed to rehearse with Rick Mascarpone—"

Stevie seemed to find this name particularly funny as well, for he chuckled freely at its mention. "Mascarpone!" he said. "Say cheese!"

"Hilarious. Now we know that Rick Mascarpone was unavailable for some reason."

"Ate too much tiramisu," suggested Stevie with a twinkle in his eye.

"So now all we need to find out is who his understudy was and we're home free," I concluded.

"I can tell you that," said Stevie. "Sam told me the other night."

"What? Why didn't you mention this before?"

"I thought you knew. It's Zack."

"Zack? What Zack?"

"Your Zack. He's the understudy for the part of Jack Mackintosh."

"You're kidding me."

"No, he was at our place the other day. He wanted to know if Sam had any tips for him. He'd never acted in a play before and Sam has, so naturally he came by to pick up some pointers."

"But it wasn't Zack. It couldn't have been."

"Yes, it was. I heard it with my own two ears." And as if to prove his point he scratched one furry appendage with his hind paw.

"He hasn't got a pimple on his nose."

"You can't hold that against him. Many people don't have pimples on their nose," explained Stevie kindly.

"The murderer!"

"What about him?"

"He's got a pimple on his nose. I saw it."

"Ah," said Stevie. "And are you sure about that, Agent Tom?"

"Of course I'm sure. A big fat pimple, right on the tip of his nose."

Stevie pawed his chin thoughtfully. These were deep waters. "Now let me get this straight. The murderer has a pimple on his nose."

"Right."

"And Zack hasn't."

"Exactly."

His face cleared. "Then it can't be Zack who viciously slew young Lucy Knicx. You must see that."

I groaned. If this was to be my life from now on, I hoped it would be over soon.

Stevie continued. He was getting into the thing now. "What this means is that there must be a third man."

"Right. A second understudy."

"Now we're finally getting somewhere, my dear Watson."

"Hey, you don't get to call me Watson. *You're* Watson in this little outfit of ours. And I'm Sherlock."

"Too bad. I've got dibs on Sherlock. You be Watson."

"No way. I'm the brains behind this operation. You're merely the 'hey you.'"

"I beg to differ, my dear Watson."

"You're doing it again!"

"Elementary, my dear—"

"Stop that."

"Now, now, my dear— Ouch!"

This last remark was in reference to the head-butt I'd given him.

"You had that coming," I said.

"Oh, all right. You can be Sherlock."

"Look, this is all wrong," I said.

"I'll say," he said, rubbing the spot where my head had collided with his.

"I don't mean that. I mean, we're not detectives. We're spies. We shouldn't model ourselves after Sherlock Holmes. We should look to James Bond as a role model."

"Right," he said, bobbing his head in agreement. "But what's the difference? I mean, we're solving a murder case, aren't we? So we're detectives, aren't we?"

"No, we're not," I said emphatically. "We're spies who just happen to solve murder cases from time to time."

"Okay," he said dubiously.

"This Lucy Knicx was probably a secret agent, murdered before she could spill the beans," I said, thinking aloud now. "I bet you a pound of chicken liver that whoever the murderer is, he's probably an enemy spy. And we," I concluded, tapping Stevie's chest, "are going to find out who's behind this."

"Oh, all right, if we must," said Stevie. He'd jumped down from the bench and was starting to wend his way towards the park exit.

"Where are you off to, then?" I said, surprised at this lack of enthusiasm for the mission.

"I'm going home," he said. "All this talk of chicken liver has made me hungry."

He had a point there. All this talk about chicken liver had made *me* hungry as well. "Mind if I join you?" I said, for I knew Father Sam didn't stint on the cat food.

"Sure," he said. "Tag along."

And tag along I did. Essential though our first spy mission was, one shouldn't lose track of the really important things in life.

15

SAM'S SELF-SERVICE

*F*ather Sam's place turned out to be a bust, though. Sneaking in through the cat flap, we were both shocked and dismayed to find that Sam had omitted to fill Stevie's cat bowl. The thing was empty! Even his water bowl was empty. And I was still shaking my head in dismay at so much negligence from a cat owner, when I noticed Father Sam had also neglected to clean out Stevie's litter box. I had trotted tither in hopes of taking a tinkle, when I saw to my disgust that the box contained at least a week's worth of Stevie's doo-doo. Yikes.

Stevie joined me with a shamefaced expression on his hairy mug. "Sorry about that," he mumbled.

"Something is very wrong here," I deduced. "Father Sam never used to be like this."

He sighed as he led me into the pantry. "I know. He's been very distracted lately. Hasn't even groomed me for ages."

I watched on as Stevie picked away at a 30 pound bag of Chicken Meal Formula. Finally the bag ripped and the wholesome grain-free and gluten-free manna from feline heaven flowed onto the floor. Stevie bade me to dig in but I insisted he go first. He was, after all, the host and I a mere guest.

His mouth full of kibble—rich in all the necessary vitamins, minerals and nutrients and recommended by the veterinary society—he said, "He's been working on the same sermon for ages."

"Must be some sermon."

"I know. And the odd thing is, he frequently locks himself up in his study and won't come out for ages. I hear him mumbling in there—probably practicing parts of his sermon —then there's the sound of crumpling paper and the wad hitting the wastepaper basket and from time to time even soft sobbing."

"That's bad," I said. "Every time Zack starts sobbing it usually means he's fallen in love again and the thing ended badly."

"Do you think Sam has fallen in love?"

I started playing with a piece of chicken-shaped kibble. "Who knows? Human males are weird that way. They'll fall in love with just about anybody."

"But Sam is no ordinary man," said Stevie. "He's a priest. They're not supposed to fall in love."

"Oh?" Of course I knew all about the topic, for Zack had once been a priest too. He's retired now, of course. Though from time to time I still catch him fingering his clerical garb when he thinks I'm not looking.

"No. Some humans—all men—pledge allegiance to another human—also a man—hanging from a cross, and from that day forward they're not allowed to even look at a woman let alone sniff her butt."

"Weird."

"Tell me about it. Imagine someone telling us not to sniff a girl's butt."

"No way."

Stevie and I pondered for a moment about the idiosyncrasies of humans. They really are a weird species. Then Stevie said something that made my ears flap. "Could you repeat that?" I said.

"I said that the girl's name is Bluebell. At least, that's the name Sam keeps mumbling when he's alone in his study working on his sermon. I put my ear to the door once and it was Bluebell this and Bluebell that the whole time. That's why I'm telling you he's fallen in love, priest or no priest."

"Bluebell," I said, frowning, for the name had rung a bell, though which one I wasn't sure yet.

"Odd name for a girl, don't you think?"

Then it struck me. Not only had Zack mentioned the name Bluebell earlier that evening, but it had also occurred in the last will and testament of the ghost of Lucy Knicx as read to me, Dana and Stevie. In my excitement I almost knocked over the entire bag of cat food. "It's a clue!" I vociferated.

"That's what I keep telling you," said Stevie with mild reproach. "Sam's gone and gotten himself entangled with some dreadful female listening to the name Bluebell. And let me tell you, Tom—can I call you Tommy?—that this spells nothing but woe, wretchedness and—"

"No, listen—"

"—worry for all involved. For once a woman enters Sam's life he won't be the Brookridge priest much longer. He'll resign or quit or whatever it is that priests do, and he'll move away from Brookridge for he won't be able to stand the disgrace and the gossip and the—"

"No, but listen—"

"—fingerpointing. We'll probably move to some ghastly back alley in some ghastly town and the new lady of the house won't like me and will kick me out of the house and I'll be forced to roam the streets where I'll suffer and struggle and die."

"But Bluebell is not a girl!" I finally managed to say.

"It's not?"

"No! Jesus, I've never met any cat who can talk so much." Apart from myself, perhaps.

"Thank you," said Stevie, and he seemed genuinely touched. "I aim to please," he added modestly.

"That's not what I meant," I started to say, then decided this wasn't an avenue I wanted to pursue with Stevie, and dropped the subject. "Zack was talking about Bluebell before—"

"Then it's definitely a girl," said Stevie. "You know what Zack is like."

I knew very well what Zack was like. In fact I think it's safe to say I'm the number one authority on all things Zack. My master, for lack of a better word, is what I would call a serial infatuator. He falls in love fast and very frequently, and whenever he starts dropping names around the house with a strange cow-like look in his eyes, I know it's that time of the month again. But this time there were extenuating circumstances.

"I do know what Zack is like, and if not for Lucy Knicx mentioning the same name in her farewell speech, I'd say you were right on the money."

There was a pause, as Stevie processed this information. I could see from the way he screwed up his face that his brain was working overtime. "Lucy Knicx?" he said finally. "Lucy Knicx mentioned the word 'Bluebell'?"

I nodded, and started striding away from the pantry. Fond though as I am of any place where the food is plenty and there simply for the taking, I thought the time had come to investigate further into this matter of Bluebell, and what better place to start than right here in Sam's place.

16

THE BLUEBELL SERMON

"*S*how me Sam's study, Watson," I said, for though I knew the Sherlock-Watson simile wasn't as pertinent as I should have liked, it still had a nice ring to it.

"So Bluebell isn't a girl, then, is she?" said Stevie, who came tripping in my wake.

"At this point in our investigation, Bluebell could be anything," I said, as we traversed the presbytery corridor. We had arrived at a sturdy oak door barring entrance into Sam's inner sanctum: his study. It was here that the great man wrote his sermons, pieces of eloquent prose that inspired the Brookridge masses week on week, or so they tell me. I must admit never having been present during Mass, cats not being allowed in Church as a rule. Not that I mind. Though Jesus was a fisherman, I have it from authoritative sources no actual fish is ever served there.

"Now what?" I said, as I gently pawed the closed door. One of the disadvantages of being a cat is that we have a hard time handling doors. Then again, one of the advantages of being a cat is that we usually find a way around this. Stevie's next words were a testament to that.

"Follow me," he said, with a roguish glint in his eye.

"Aye, aye, sir," I said. We were in Stevie's lair now, and even though I had my doubts about my new partner's intelligence, he wouldn't be much of a cat if he didn't now the ins and outs of his own place. He led me up a creaking staircase covered with a worn-out oriental runner. On the landing he disappeared into a bathroom that had also seen better days and hopped onto the toilet seat. From there he took a quick leap and disappeared into an opening in the wall where once a vent had been.

"Are you coming?" his voice echoed from inside the wall.

"Yup," I said, and in two bounds I had joined him. We were now inside the wood paneled wall and were heading South again. As I took in the sights—dust and mouse droppings—I asked him the one question that had been on the forefront on my mind. "Any good mice around here?"

"Nah," he said, looking over his shoulder before taking a leap from one supporting beam to the next. "Sam's a great Christian, or at least that's what everyone tells me, but the part of his scripture about turning the other cheek, doesn't seem to apply to mice. He's managed to chase them all away by putting mousetraps everywhere. Word about these heavy-handed tactics spread fast—mouse to mouse so to speak—and pretty soon they stopped coming."

I shook my weary head. This deplorable attitude towards members of the rodent population pained me and I said as much.

"I know," he said, with a dejected twitch of his tail. "But what can you do? I rip open a garbage bag once in a while, but before the little buggers can catch a whiff of the stuff, Sam has fixed them with one of his traps. Ah, here we are."

He slid gracefully through a small crack in the wall and we came out behind an old gas stove in the corner of what I assumed to be Father Sam's famous study. Instantly Stevie hopped up onto an outsized desk taking up most of the space, and I took a closer look at that wastepaper basket Stevie had been telling me so much about. The one with all the discarded drafts of his sermon.

"Nothing here," said Stevie from his perch on top of the desk. In the meantime I was having better luck sorting through Sam's trash. I had smoothed out a few of his crumpled drafts and my eye had spied the magic word not once but dozens of times on every page: Bluebell was pretty much ubiquitous. I read the first sentence aloud—yes, cats can read. You didn't know that, did you?

"Oh, my love. I yearn for you with every fiber of my being. I lust for you with every corpuscle in my body. I long to hold you in my arms and hug you, caress you, kiss you, love you with every—"

"Please," said Stevie, holding up a paw. "If you don't want a mess on the carpet better stop it right there." He made a gagging sound and I saw what he meant. It was pretty soppy stuff.

"Um…" I hesitated to clothe my next thought into words. "Are you sure this is the draft of a sermon?"

"Of course it is. Sam doesn't work on anything else. He's devoted to his flock."

I pursed my lips. I'd heard of a priest's devotion to his parishioners before, but this was really taking things to the next level. I tried to break it gently. "Sounds to me like a love letter, Steve."

Stevie let out an agonized wail. "So it is true after all! The silly goop has gone and fallen in love with some ghastly female. I knew it!"

I didn't know what to say. "Tough luck," I finally managed to mumble, and put a comforting paw on Stevie's back. I sympathized with the poor sod, having gone through the same horrifying experience many times myself. In fact every time Zack falls in love—once a month, like clockwork—I fret and worry until the danger passes. Luckily so far it always has, but one never knows that some day some half-witted member of the opposite sex will take a fancy to the silly poop, move in and boot me out on my red fanny. I suppressed a shiver at the mere thought.

"I'm done for," sighed Stevie, stooping his shoulders in dejection.

"Yah, well..." Then something occurred to me. "Look, have you ever seen the wench? I mean, actually seen her come round here?"

Stevie shook his head. "Only Zada Sellar drops in from time to time. She's one of Sam's most faithful parishioners. And Mathilda Bladder of course. Chairwoman of the church council. But as far as I can tell Sam has never harbored any romantic notions about either of them."

Since Zada Sellar is about a hundred years old and Mathilda Bladder the worst gossipmonger Brookridge has ever harbored, this didn't surprise me. "It occurs to me that perhaps it's not too late yet. I mean, if he's still in the writing stage of the proceedings, it stands to reason nothing has happened yet."

He looked at me with hope and confusion nicely blended in his clear blue eyes. "What do you mean?"

"Well, you know how it goes. When humans fall in love they start writing letters, dozens of them, each one soupier than the next."

"Like this one." He pawed the exhibit with distaste.

"Exactly. But this is only in the early stages of the disease. Once the virus spreads, and they've gone on several dates together, there's the kissing stage—"

He closed his eyes. "Please. Spare me the details."

"—and then, finally, they move in together."

69

His tail quavered visibly. "Must you remind me?" he said, pained.

"All I mean to say is that the letter-writing stage is usually situated somewhere between the kissing stage and the cohabitation stage. Which means…"

His eyes lit up. "Which means there's still hope!"

"Sure there is," I said encouragingly.

"And then there's the fact that Zack was also murmuring the ghastly female's name."

I started at these words. I'd forgotten all about that. "I wouldn't exactly say murmuring," I corrected this misinterpretation of the facts pertaining to the case.

"I do say murmuring," he went on. "And I'll say more. Zack can't stop thinking about the Bluebell menace, Sam can't stop writing her long and ghastly letters and Lucy Knicx mentions her as she heaves her dying breath—"

"It wasn't her dying breath," I corrected him once again. "She was already dead."

"Still."

"Still," I agreed. He had a point there. Now that I came to think about it, Zack had indeed muttered the Bluebell name like he does when he's just fallen truly, madly, deeply in love again.

"I'll bet you a can of tuna that the Bluebell is one of those *femme fatales* who waltz into a place and leave a pile of dead bodies and broken hearts in their wake."

"You know what?" I said, musing. "I think you're on to something there, Agent Steve."

"Of course I'm onto something," he said very immodestly. "And you know what we're going to do, Agent Tom? We're going to find out who this Bluebell dame is and put a stop to this femme fataling she's been doing." He extended a claw. "One. We solve the Lucy Knicx murder, which is probably some sort of *crime passionnel*."

I was impressed Stevie had words like *crime passionnel* in his vocabulary.

He extended a second claw. "Two. We drive the Bluebell out of town and…" He extended a third claw. "… three. We save our homes from being wrecked and our butts from being evicted. What do you say?"

I had to hand it to him. It sounded like a good scheme. I only saw one flaw. "How are we going to drive La Bluebell out of Brookridge?"

He deflated a little. "That's… something we need to think about."

"Let's first find out more about her, shall we?" I suggested. "We can figure out the rest as we go along." I still thought the girl was an enemy spy but since I didn't want to blow Stevie's bubble, I refrained from saying so.

"Great scheme!" he said.

And it was as we sat congratulating one another on a fine piece of espionage work, that the door suddenly opened and Sam walked in.

17

SAM THE NIGHT CRAWLER

I don't know if you've ever noticed how cats have these soft pads under their paws? You have? Then you probably also know what they're there for. Not to hurt ourselves when we land? Whoever gave you that idea? No, the reason we have those nifty little pink cushions is so we can quickly and quietly sneak out of the room whenever a human catches us doing something we're not supposed to. That's why, when Sam suddenly surprised us by bursting into his study, we were safely behind the gas stove before he so much as had an inkling we were ever there.

"What is he doing here?" I hissed, as I darted a quick glance from behind the stove.

"He lives here," hissed back Stevie reasonably, and I saw his point.

From our hiding place we could see how Sam was staring at the love letters I'd smoothed out and laid side by side on the carpet.

"Dammit," I groaned, for I'd completely forgotten the cardinal rule of espionage: never leave a trace behind.

"Too late now," said Stevie, as he eyed every move of his master in tense concentration.

Father Sam Malone was a handsome fellow, as men go, or at least that's what I keep hearing from my female associates. He's tall, lean and muscular, with the kind of chiseled features and full head of hair most commonly found on the covers on display in the supermarket romance novel section. The fact that Brookridge is one of those small towns where the church still fills up nicely every Sunday morning attests to the man's powers of attraction. That the force is strong in this one, is attested to by the fact that it's mostly women occupying the pews and hanging on every word that rolls from this wonder man's sensual lips—don't blame me for this last adjective. Blame Dana, for she's the one nauseating me with that description of the man's chops. She also told me the padre's got a nice singing voice, though that's probably neither here nor there. He was now looking slightly disheveled, as if he'd just rolled out of bed, which he probably had.

Sam was now collecting the fruits of his penmanship with trembling hands and laid them carefully on his desk. He stood staring at them for a space, probably wondering what had induced him to destroy them in the first place, when it was so obvious fate wanted them preserved for posterity, then he heaved a deep sigh and uttered the single word both me and Stevie had come to dread: "Bluebell."

"Oh, my God," moaned Stevie.

"You can say that again," I muttered.

Something of our verbal utterances must have reached the good father's ears, for he turned to stare in our direction. Then Stevie, the mutt, couldn't resist the temptation of a cuddle, and walked over to his master to stroke himself against the latter's leg.

I groaned at the sight of an agent giving free rein to his

baser impulses. And I was just making a mental note of this utterly unprofessional behavior on the part of my new partner, when the telephone rang. The sound seemed to startle Sam—a clear sign of a bad conscience—and it was with marked nervousness that he picked up the receiver. Then again, since the night was now well advanced, he was probably simply wondering who the hell was phoning him at this hour.

"Hello?" he said tentatively, as if expecting someone to jump from the earpiece and snap his head off. Then he visibly relaxed and took a seat at the desk. "Oh, it's you. What do you want? Yeah? Well, you're not going to get it."

Very mysterious, all this, don't you think? At least I thought so, and so did Stevie, for he threw questioning glances in my direction. I merely shrugged, indicating I, too, had no idea what was going on.

Meanwhile Sam had risen, and so had his temper. "Then tell him I'm in charge here and if he doesn't like, he can lump it!" he said in the tones of one who's had about all he can take and can't take no more. "Now listen here, you... you... Hello? Hello? Hell and damnation!"

And on this last word, he slammed down the receiver. It doesn't often happen that you see a man of God lose it like that, and the spectacle was a fascinating one, to be honest.

"Who does he think he is, calling me up in the middle of the night?"

The voice intruded upon my reverie and for a moment I wondered where it had come from. It sounded like Father Sam, only more subdued somehow, as if spoken in an undertone.

"I'm in charge and I don't have to take this."

Once again I had the impression Sam had spoken, only this time I'd been watching him carefully, and his lips hadn't moved! I threw a quick glance over at Stevie, to see if he was experiencing the same phenomenon, but my Ragamuffin friend was licking his butt, lost to the world.

"Next time he phones I'll tell him his suggestions stink. That's right. Stink. Ha! That'll teach him."

A jagged lump that seemed to have inserted itself into my throat prevented me from crying out in terrified horror, and I swallowed it down with some effort. My eyes and ears hadn't deceived me: I was hearing Sam, even though he wasn't speaking!

18

READING MINDS

"*Now* where did I put that final draft?" Sam thought, as he started rifling through his desk drawers.

As clear as if he was enunciating the words, I could hear Sam's every single thought! I sat staring at the man from my hiding place, slowly shaking my head. This wasn't possible. This wasn't... Then I remembered something Dana had said. Something about planting thoughts in people's heads. Could it be? Nah, of course not. Or could it?

"Ah, here it is. Now where were we? Mh, yes. Jack Mackintosh is relaxing in his den, watching a game, when suddenly the doorbell rings. He goes to open the door and finds Zoe hovering on the mat. He quickly steps outside, trying to induce the girl to take a hike, when..."

My eyes were bubbling and my ears were ringing. This wasn't really happening. And yet it was.

Sam had taken out a pencil and was jotting down notes in the margin. "Mrs Mackintosh isn't home," he was saying to himself. "So why doesn't Jack invite Zoe in?" He sat back in his chair, and tapped the pencil thoughtfully on his papers.

"Of course. He doesn't want the neighbors to see." He smiled and wrote another note as he stuck out his tongue and spelled the note in his head. "He doesn't want the neighbors to know about the affair. Especially Mrs. Mueller. There. Not bad." A wide smile creased his face as he admired his own cleverness. "I'm so smart!" he thought.

For a moment I'd had the distinct sensation I was going mad, but now I knew this was really happening; only humans could act this silly.

"Jesus, I'm clever!" the man was thinking.

"Jesus, he's an idiot!" I was thinking.

"I'm a frickin' genius!" Sam thought.

"He's a frickin' moron!" I thought.

"I'm hungry," Stevie thought.

It was the first thought of Stevie's that had penetrated my consciousness, and I only had two answers as to why that was: either Sam's mental processes had dominated my cerebral cortex to the exclusion of all else, or Stevie simply didn't think all that much. I leaned towards the latter, especially since Stevie's next thought was, "I wonder what tastes better, left chicken breast or right chicken breast?"

I was drowning in a sea of imbecility and for a moment toyed with the idea of simply exiting the scene stage left, then fought down the inclination and decided to hang in there, lest I missed vital information pertaining to the case.

Father Sam seemed to have exhausted his creative faculties, for he threw what I now knew to be the screenplay for Murder in the Park on his desk, raked his fingers through his hair, and thought, "Better get some more sleep. Beddy-bye-bye, baby."

He flicked off the light in the room and stumbled out, presumably back to bed. I shook my head, dazed and confused.

"Did you hear that?" I said, leaving my perch behind the stove to confer with my fellow espionage expert.

"Huh?" said Stevie intelligently. "What's that?" he added for good measure.

"Didn't you hear what Sam just thought?" I specified my question, though from Stevie's vacuous expression I already had my answer.

"How would I know what Sam thought? I'm not a mind reader."

Reluctant though I was to pursue a line of questioning fraught with embarrassment, I persisted. "Didn't you hear..." For a moment I struggled with myself, then I was strong again. "... beddy-bye-bye?"

"Betty who?"

"Forget about it."

"Is she Bob the butcher's fine feline?"

"No, she is not," I said rather more fiercely than I should have.

"Oh. All right."

Just my luck, I thought, that Dana would saddle me up with the biggest boob this side of Brookridge.

"I resent that," the boob now said.

I started. He couldn't have heard what I just thought? "What?"

"That wisecrack about me being the biggest boob this side of Brookridge," he said, sounding wounded. "I may be a boob but I'm sure there are bigger boobs out there."

"D-did you hear that?"

He eyed me censoriously. "Nothing wrong with my ears, you know."

"But I didn't speak."

"Sure you did."

"No, I didn't. It was just a thought."

"That's all right. I forgive you."

"A thought that I didn't say out loud," I said with some exasperation.

Once again he eyed me dubiously. "Look, I may not be the smartest cat on the block, but that's no reason to keep joshing me."

"I'm not joshing you. Here, watch my lips."

"Why would I want to watch your... Hey!" He now stared at me, wide-eyed, as if he'd seen the ghost of Lucy Knicx, for I'd just formulated the thought that a right-winged chicken's right breast was probably meatier than its left breast due to the muscular development in the favored limb.

"How do you know I was thinking about chicken breasts?" he said, somewhat flabbergasted. Then a second thought crushed into the first. "And why can I hear you even though your lips aren't moving?"

I put a comforting paw on his shoulder. "Buddy, I think we're in for a world of weirdness. You and I are now able to read minds."

He shrugged off my paw and licked he spot where it'd been placed. "Read minds? Are you nuts? And stop doing that!"

I had just thought that if I was nuts, so was Stevie. "I'm not doing anything. I'm just thinking."

"Then don't!"

Well, you know how it is. Tell someone not to think about pink elephants, and the thought will spring up like lilies of the valley come springtime. For a moment silent reigned while thousands of thoughts simultaneously crashed into my consciousness, 50 percent mine and the other half Stevie's. We both groaned an agonized groan as our synapses fired on all cylinders.

"It's the FSA," I finally managed to say over the din, and instantly the mental noise died down. "Hey, when I speak I don't think."

He looked at me keenly. "I notice. It's as if the volume knob is suddenly turned all the way down."

"Looks like the trick is to keep talking," I said.

"Not a problem for me," he said, bright-eyed.

"So Dana wasn't pulling my leg when she fed me all that stuff about planting thoughts in humans," I mused.

"We can plant thoughts in humans?" Stevie said with sudden enthusiasm.

"Be forewarned, Agent Steve," I said sternly. "Our powers are given us to aid and protect the human race, not induce them to provide us with more and better kibble."

"Oh, all right," muttered Stevie. "Though if I could just plant one teensiest tiniest suggestion that he switch brands? He's been buying me the same brand of chicken for three years now, and I'd give my right paw to have a change of menu once in a while. I mean, how long can you keep eating the same thing over and over and over—"

"Yeah, yeah," I said, interrupting what promised to be a lengthy harangue about the pros and cons of the different brands of cat food. "I wonder who that call came from…"

"Can't you go upstairs and plant a thought in Sam's head that he needs to give you the name of his correspondent?" suggested Stevie.

It was not a bad idea, I mused.

"Thanks," said Stevie. "I do get them from time to time."

Dang, if my fellow agent was going to read my mind the whole time, there was nothing I'd be able to keep a secret from him anymore. Not that I had such big secrets to hide, but one does like to harbor one's little mysteries.

"Don't worry," he said, as if he'd read my mind, which he had. "I won't tell a soul." And he gave me a fat wink that almost made me slap him over the head.

19

DREAMS

*B*efore we snuck upstairs to perform our FSA brand of brain surgery on Father Sam and discover all his secrets, I quickly perused the Murder in the Park script lying on the priest's desk for any clues pertaining to the case. What I was most curious about was the Zoe Huckleberry-Jack Mackintosh scene I'd been a prime witness to.

As I'd suspected, the scene didn't end with a large butcher's knife being strategically placed between the Huckleberry shoulder blades but rather with a prolonged kissing sequence that would have all the female audience members heave with delight. The bepimpled murderer had definitely missed out on a good thing.

The one thing conspicuously missing from the screenplay was any reference to this mysterious Bluebell, whoever of whatever it might be.

I closed the script with a frown, now wondering who would replace Lucy Knicx in the play, which I knew to premiere in one week if all went well.

"I can tell you that," said Stevie, who had been closely

81

following my thought processes. "Jamie Burrow from next door was Lucy Knicx's understudy, so it stands to reason she'll take over as Zoe whatsername."

"Huckleberry," I said automatically. "You know this Burrow girl?"

Stevie, who'd sat licking his belly—you don't retain that snowy-white complexion without a goodish amount of grooming—inclined his red-whiskered head. "Sure I do. Comes round here all the time. She used to be a choirgirl and an acolyte when she was little." He grinned. "She's not so little anymore, though. Quite the catch, apparently. Not that I would know about these things," he quickly added. "But as the parish cat one hears rumors, doesn't one?"

"One certainly does," I assented, making a mental note about Jamie Burrow's essential catchness.

Since Father Sam had left the study door open, we didn't have any walls to scale or acrobatic feats to perform to reach his upstairs bedroom and sneak in. We both took a seat on the bedside mat and stared up at the figure lying not three feet away. Apart from the fact that Sam was softly snoring and that he drooled in his sleep, at first glance there wasn't much information to glean. I actually didn't catch a single thought at first.

"Are you picking up anything?" I thought.

"Not a peep," Stevie thought. "No, wait. He's thinking something. A red clown is jumping through a yellow hoop and bowing to thunderous applause from a massive audience."

I was also getting this. "Probably a dream," I thought. "The clown is probably Sam, and the audience his congregation."

"Yes," thought Stevie thoughtfully, "but then why is the clown buck naked all of a sudden and trying desperately to hide behind the podium curtains?"

"Stage fright," I thought. "Typical Freudian stuff. Father Sam must suffer from some form of stage fright. It can't be easy standing in front of a congregation every week and having to come up with a fresh sermon each time."

"I think it's that play," thought Stevie. "Ever since they asked him to be the director, he hasn't been himself. Fretting, moody, jumpy. Like you saw, he even forgets to put out my food."

"At least it wasn't a love letter he was writing, but merely the script for the play."

We watched on as Sam slept. I really wanted to plant a thought in his head but since Dana had summarily dismissed us from the Brookridge Park crime scene without giving any further instructions or even a time table for our FSA agent training, I had no idea how. The mind reading thing was something we'd accidentally stumbled upon, but I had the distinct impression planting thoughts in people's heads required more skill than we possessed.

"Who was the man who called you?" I mentally projected at Sam's inert form. "Who was that man on the phone?" Or, more important still, "Who is the man with the pimple?" And, most importantly, "Who is Bluebell?"

But no thought emanated from Sam other than that the clown had now discovered a trap door on stage and was lowering himself through it in order to affect his escape. Raucous laughter from the audience spurred him on, and after a last wave and a sad smile, he dropped himself through the hatch and was gone.

"Discouraging," whispered Stevie, returning to a more classic mode of conversation. "The man is impervious to our methods of interrogation."

I sighed. "Impervious is right."

"Perhaps if we wait long enough, something will come up? I mean, it's not as if we have somewhere to be."

Once again my esteemed colleague was right. There was nowhere else to go and nothing else to investigate right now. Brookridge Park was off limits, and the only other person who could shed some light on the Bluebell mystery was Zack, who was also fast asleep. But waiting by his side or continuing our Sam vigil amounted to the same thing.

"Let's make it a night out with the boys!" whispered Stevie, after I'd mentally consented to his idea. "I'll bring the kibble, you bring the milk."

"And how am I supposed to do that?" I said, already regretting the whole scheme.

Stevie scratched his scalp. "I hadn't thought of that."

"I know."

The night went as most nights do: uneventful to a degree. I would have liked to say we came up with some great new insights into the mind of man, or some clue or vital piece of evidence that solved the whole mystery with a snap, but it didn't exactly turn out this way.

As far as insights into the human psyche go, after the clown episode Sam went on to dream about a frog reciting a poem in front of a crowd of thousands, and suddenly noticing he hasn't brought his hat. Feeling terribly naked without his hat, he then hops off the stage, leaving the crowd roaring with laughter. So yeah, the guy definitely had issues. But since I'm not the Freudster, they didn't really grip me.

Frankly, by the time he started dreaming about a rabbit, standing in front of a football stadium and reading from his collected works during the break, I called it quits.

"Hey, where are you going?" said Stevie, who was following the rabbit story with rapt attention.

"I'm going home," I said.

"But don't you want to know how the story ends?"

"It starts to rain. The rabbit discovers he came out without his umbrella. He disappears into a left field rabbit hole. The crowd laughs its collective fanny off. See ya later, partner."

Stevie, who was still tuned into Sam's reveries, turned to me with an awed expression on his mug. "You're right!" he said. "It just started to rain! How did you know?"

I merely gave a tired shrug. Though sitting up nights is a mainstay of any cat's life, it usually doesn't involve having to psychoanalyze a sleeping man's dream world. Somehow it just didn't feel right, intruding upon his private space like that. And it sure as heck didn't feel productive.

I ambled through Father Sam's small vegetable garden—tomatoes and lettuce—as the sun slowly rose, heralding a new and glorious day for all of Brookridge—and probably the rest of the word as well, though that was of no concern to me, per se. I stretched, arching my back, and wondered when I'd hear from Dana. Considering the fact that both Stevie and I featured pretty low on the FSA totem pole, I had a feeling this would be later rather than sooner. She was probably too busy solving the Brookridge Park murder case. Or had perhaps already solved it. She and her three Peterbald heavies.

By now she had probably planted the information about the man-with-the-pimple in Bart Ganglion's policeman's brain and that most capable officer had made an arrest and the case of Lucy Knicx's unfortunate demise was closed.

I yawned; what did I expect? That two rookies, not even having started on their first day of spy school, would crack this case wide open? Fat chance. I strolled homeward, passing the back yards of the few houses that stood between Father Sam's presbytery and the end of Tulip Street, and was once again on familiar turf: Bellflower Street. I passed through the back yards of Tanner Tompon's place, Terrell McCrady and Lexie Moonstone's dwelling, and past Royce Moppett's house. And this is where the trouble began.

As you may or may not know, Royce Moppett is the human who once must have made a grave error in a previous life. Whether it was accidentally poisoning his King and Queen whilst working as a castle cook or invading the wrong country whilst crusading for the Pope, Karma, that humorless equalizer, has now saddled him with the dubious honor of being the caretaker of Brutus, that blot on the Brookridge scene. And Brutus, having not much else to do than bully his own kind, is always on the prowl for potential victims. He was so now, for I hadn't crossed halfway through the Moppett yard, when his raspy voice rang out behind me.

"Where do you think you're going, meatball?"

20

BRUTUS HAS A THEORY

I sagged a little, for the last thing I wanted now was to get into a tussle with that horrid Persian. "Just passing through," I said casually, as I picked up my pace. Once in my own garden, Brutus usually backs off. Zack has a way of chasing him away that doesn't appeal to the big brute's sense of self-esteem. No bully likes to be bullied by the bigger bully. Not that Zack is a bully, but he is big, and he hates Moppett's guts, a sentiment he courteously extends to all things Moppett, including Brutus.

I was just about to hop through the fence to the safety of my own yard, when Brutus cut me off. He's one of those cats who likes to play with his victims before pouncing on them. Much the same way I like to play with a mouse before… Now that I come to think of it, perhaps this, once again, is Karma at work?

"Tell me something," Brutus snarled, blocking my safe passage. "Have you told anyone about our little conversation?"

I frowned. "What conversation?" So much had happened that night that I honestly didn't remember.

He looked none too pleased at the deficiency of my memory. "The ghost," he barked. "The napmares I've been having about the dead broad. You remember? You told me to see Dana about them."

"Oh, that's right," I said, greatly relieved. "You did tell me about those." I now realized that Brutus seemed oddly perplexed. And what I'd mistaken for his usual ruffian demeanor was merely a front to hide his perturbation at a phenomenon he didn't understand and therefore feared.

"Well, I went to see Dana."

"And how did it go?"

"Not too well," he said gruffly, as he stared at his paws. "She was with three ugly-looking brutes who told me to take a hike the moment I approached her. Dana herself was busy, she said, and if I could come back some other time. Too busy," he scoffed. "Can you beat it? Too busy to help out her fellow cat?"

"I met those Peterbalds," I said, for lack of anything better to say. "They're not nice."

"Not nice! That's the understatement of the year, buddy!"

It was the first time that Brutus had ever referred to me with this epitaph, which was definitely a step up from his usual meatball or fathead. I didn't know what to say. "Yeah, well…"

"Those guys are animals," he said, and his voice suddenly took on a conspiratorial note. "I bet they come from Southridge."

It's one of those facts of life that, faced with a common enemy, old enemies become friends. Southridge is our neighboring town, and whenever bad things happen in Brookridge, the blame invariably falls on Southridge.

"I bet they do," I said. I had a theory that the Peterbalds were probably manufactured in a secret FSA lab somewhere, but I refrained from voicing this idea. I was, after all, an FSA agent now, and even though I had yet to sign a formal agreement, I was presumably bound by a long list of confidentiality clauses and whatnot.

"And I'll tell you another thing," he said, still in that same undertone. "Dana's gone and gotten herself mixed up in some really weird stuff. And I think it's up to her friends to get her out of it."

I winced. Had Brutus just called me his friend? As I said, it had been a long night and I was tired, so perhaps I hadn't heard him right. "You mean…"

He nodded emphatically. "You and me, buddy. We've got to get from under that nasty Southridge spell. Dana's a Brookridge girl, and I'll be damned if I'll allow those monsters to possess her."

"Possess her?"

"Sure. I haven't figured out exactly how they do it, but somehow they've managed to take over her mind. Dana's a sweet girl. Not too bright. And those are usually the first victims. Then, knowing I'd never stand for it, they've started directing their mind altering techniques on me. That's why I've been having these napmares, see? All part of their plan."

"Which is?"

He moved closer and I now found myself face to face with my former nemesis. It was not an agreeable experience. For one thing, the cat's eyes were positively burning with a strange fire. "Which is to lay claim to all of Brookridge's natural resources. Starting, of course, with our queens."

"You don't say."

"I just did. And I'll say more. I'm certain those three bald uglies are only the vanguard. The worst is yet to come."

21

AN UNEXPECTED PARTNERSHIP

*B*rutus suddenly thrust out a paw. I stared at it blankly.

"Tap it," he urged. I tapped it. Reluctantly, for I've never been fond of physical contact with the brute.

"It's imperative that we join forces, my friend," he now said. "United we stand. Divided we fall. And all that jazz."

When cats of Brutus's ilk start using ten-dollar words like imperative, something's definitely off. "Right," I mumbled, and started to inch my way towards the hedge dividing our gardens once again.

He cut off my retreat by slinging an arm around my neck and dragging me along towards a small but hideous fountain neighbor Moppett has erected in the center of his garden. I'd seen Brutus hovering near the thing before. He's one of those cats that like water, and he enjoys the spray of the fountain on his coat. Now, I also like water, but not in the company of my least favorite cat in the world.

He invited me to take a seat on top of the stone bench Moppett has placed next to the fountain by giving me a hard shove in the rear.

"Hop it," he said curtly, when I displayed a certain hesitation.

I hopped it, and now found myself staring out at two fat little limestone angels spewing water into a limestone bowl and onto the two of us.

"We need to devise a strategy," said Brutus, making himself comfortable and lifting his face to enjoy the droplets falling on his fur and whiskers. "Ah, that's the life," he murmured, then shook himself with relish. "I can't tell you how horrible those dreams have been. There's that woman, completely drenched, and she keeps staring at me, pointing an accusing finger, and saying 'You should have saved me, little one. You should have saved me when you had the chance.' Pretty scary stuff."

His story had shaken me profoundly. This was the exact same thing that had happened to me, right down to the phrasing. Was Lucy Knicx still at it? And why would she appear to Brutus? He hadn't been there when she was murdered. Why would she blame him of all cats of what had happened?

"When was the last time you... saw her?" I said.

"Oh, just now," he said. "I was having a nap when I suddenly woke up and saw you trespassing—I mean, passing through. And good thing you did, because I was having a doozy." He shivered. "The ghost lady was at it again, as usual, but this time there was some guy in the picture as well. Standing behind her with a big, shiny knife in his hand. And it looked like he meant business."

I sat up a little straighter. "A guy? What did he look like?"

Brutus eyed me strangely. "What does it matter what he looked like? Some human, you know. They all look alike to me."

"Did he have..." I hesitated, wondering how I was going to explain this.

"Did he have what?" said Brutus, some of his old peeve returning.

"Did he have a big, fat pimple right on the tip of his nose?" I said, taking the plunge.

"So you have been having the same dreams!" he exclaimed, giving me a clap on the back that almost landed me right in the middle of the fountain.

Teetering on the edge of the bench for a moment, I managed to retain my balance and grinned at my newest friend. "Yep, same dreams."

He frowned at the memory of the dreams he'd been sharing with yours truly. "Ugly-looking brute," he growled. "Even without that fat pimple. Though he does remind me of someone I know."

I pricked up my ears. This was news. "Oh?"

"Yeah. Some fellow who's been hanging around the park these last couple months. Though this one didn't have a pimple now that I come to think of it."

"Pimples come and go," I said.

"They do, don't they?" he agreed. "I remember Royce once had a pimple the size of the Atomium on his schnoz. He tried everything to get rid of the thing, since Rose wouldn't allow him out of the house until it was gone." He cackled with delight at the memory. "It finally subsided after one week, just in time for the annual neighborhood barbecue."

Rose Moppett, I have to explain, is very particular about appearances, and likes both herself and her husband to appear their very best when stepping out, a policy she unfortunately also extends to Brutus, for the foul brute invariably looks like he just stepped off the front cover of The Cat Times. He was licking his belly, still chuckling fruitily about Royce's pimple, when I interrupted him. "That pimpled fellow is the ghost woman's murderer," I said, returning his attention to the matter at hand.

He looked up, interested. "I thought as much," he said keenly, "when I saw him wielding that big knife behind her back."

"And it's my belief," I continued, "that only when we figure out who the murderer is, and bring him to justice, these napmares will stop."

"You do, do you?" he said, swatting at a fly with his tail. He nodded thoughtfully. "I see your point. We revenge her murder so she can rest in peace. Very clever, fathead—I mean, Tom. Did you think of this yourself?"

"All by myself," I said with understandable pride.

He let his eye wander over me as if seeing me in an entirely new light. He must have liked what he saw, for at the end of this inspection, he grinned. A ghastly sight. "All right, then. I guess that makes us partners."

I started violently. "P-p-partners?" I said, shaken.

"Of course. I'll admit you've got brains, meatb— I mean, Tom, but I've got the brawn. Together we'll solve this murder in no time. You'll figure out the identity of the pimpled killer, and I'll take him out."

"Take him out?" I couldn't believe what I was hearing. Cats don't take out humans. It's simply not done. Furthermore, I was now an FSA agent, and sworn to protect humans, not harm them, even if they did prove to be cold-blooded killers. "But we can't take the law into our own paws," I said.

"Why not? Easy as chicken pie. You just find out who this knife-wielding maniac is, and I'll do the rest..." He punched me lightly on the shoulder. "Partner."

"But—"

He yawned cavernously. "I'm off. Got a hot date with a pillow. Just let me know when you've got the fellow in your sights and I'll be there." And sliding gracefully from the bench, he left me to ruminate on the consequences of this new alliance.

As far as I could see I was now partnered up to the hilt with not one but two undesirables. Though I had to admit Stevie was growing on me. Throughout our nightly vigil I had even grown to like the hairy blabbermouth. I just wondered how he would respond to this sudden extension of our duo to a trio. On the other hand, seeing as this espionage business could get dangerous, perhaps it wasn't such a bad idea to have a known strongcat on our team. If Dana had her Peterbalds, we had Brutus. And though I was still feeling positively dubious about this latest development, it was with a lighter heart that I descended from the Moppett bench and made my way home.

22

DANA DROPS BY

*A*rriving home, I did the eating and drinking bit, but somehow that didn't satisfy me. And as I munched down another piece of kibble, I remembered how Zack always likes to sleep late. Perhaps if I could just test my 'planting thoughts' abilities on him for a bit, I could find out some more about the mystery that was puzzling me. I would never say a bad word about the guy—he is, after all, the hand that feeds—but it is a well-established fact in Brookridge that Zack is not exactly the sharpest tool in the shed. And I had this theory that his weaker intellect would yield more readily to my newfound powers of psychic persuasion.

I trotted upstairs and found my lord and master tangled up in his bed sheets, as usual. I hopped up on the bed and made myself comfortable at the foot, where Zack has placed a sheet for me. I first scanned his dreams. Not surprisingly, they dealt mainly with food and women, Zack's two main interests in life. At this moment the Don Juan was entertaining a remarkably pretty girl during dinner in some fancy restaurant. Unlike real life, Zack had the girl in convulsions by directing at her an endless stream of witty banter, while dozens of waiters hurried to and fro, carrying laden trays with the most delicious foodstuffs imaginable. Talk about wishful dreaming.

Unfortunately, the dream held Zack so strongly in its grip that when I tried to introduce the Bluebell theme into the conversation, it was met with a stoic refusal. I tried again, by whispering the curious name in Zack's mental ear, but the waiters kept on strewing roast chicken from their proverbial hats and Zack moved his odd brand of eloquence into higher gear by asking the girl if she liked cats and, being informed that she did, starting waxing eloquent on... me.

I was touched, of course, and since it's always nice to listen to a seemingly endless stream of compliments, I momentarily lost all interest in the mission and drifted off into a refreshing sleep, myself. I don't know what *I* dreamt about, but I have a hunch it had something to do with being the birthday cat at some fancy dinner party thrown in my honor.

It was probably late when I woke up, what with having been through the most eventful night in my young life. And what woke me wasn't the chirping of the birds or Zack heaving his large frame out of bed, but the sensation that someone was staring at me. When I opened my eyes I discovered I wasn't far from the truth: Dana was sitting not three feet away from me, studying me intently.

"Huh?" I said, my keen feline brain springing into action.

She merely shook her head in what I would describe as a censorious fashion.

"What's going on?" I said, as I smacked my lips and suppressed a yawn.

"How you can sleep, at a time like this, is beyond me," were her opening words.

I shook my head to clear out the cobwebs. I know you humans like to think cats are never fully asleep, that our razor sharp senses are constantly on the alert, that with the flick of a claw we are wide awake, ready to face any danger, and respond to any contingency with an alacrity that seems almost preternatural.

While this is perhaps the case with most cats, I like to put in my twenty hours of shut-eye and prefer not to be disturbed while doing so. FSA principals bothering me at home while I'm catching my Z's are not well received, and I gave Dana both the glare and the puckered face as I tried to adjust my faculties.

Perhaps it's living with a notorious lazybones like Zack that has eroded my natural impulses, but I like to think sleep is a necessary instrument for restoring the tissues and keeping oneself functioning at top level.

"What do you want?" I said, not enjoying this habit of Dana's to give me the third degree every time we met.

"Something has happened," she said, still staring at me with that look of mild reproach.

"So?" I said. "Something always does."

"There's been a second murder."

23

STARTLING REVELATIONS

I started. "What? Where? When?"

"Last night, while you were sleeping," she said tersely.

I drew myself up to my full height. "I wasn't sleeping last night," I said with as much hauteur as I could manage on the spur of the moment. "I was… investigating."

She scoffed. "Of course you were."

"I was!" I exclaimed, now truly offended. Not only had this cat the gall to enter my personal space uninvited, she came loaded with all kinds of unfounded accusations. "In fact, Stevie and I discovered several extremely valuable clues!"

She seemed unimpressed. "And did any of those 'extremely valuable clues' point to the Brookridge Park serial killer?"

I gulped. "Serial killer?"

She nodded. "The same thing happened again. Under the same tree."

"But how do you know it was the same guy?"

"Because someone saw what happened and described the

killer as a fellow with a large and distinct pimple on the nose. Furthermore, he and the victim—a girl named Jamie Burrow —were practicing what sounds like the same scene from the Murder in the Park play, when he suddenly took out a big, shiny knife from the recesses of his costume and laid into her."

"Oh, no!" I exclaimed.

"Oh, yes," she said, a twinge of pain now marring her furry face.

"Jamie Burrow... she was Lucy Knicx's understudy for the Zoe Huckleberry part."

She looked up, surprised. "How do you know?"

"Stevie and I paid a visit to Father Sam's study last night— he's directing the play, you know—and Stevie said Jamie Burrow would be replacing Lucy in the play. She'd been coming by a couple of times."

Dana looked up at this, visibly surprised, then nodded. "Come with me. There's something I want to show you."

"Oh, all right," I said, as casually as I could, though inwardly I felt as proud as a peacock. Seems like those Peter-balds didn't give full satisfaction after all. Of course, that's what you get when hiring the pure muscle: all brawn and no brains. Then, since thinking about brawn and brains reminded me too much of my recent encounter with Brutus, I banished all thoughts of muscle heads altogether and focused on Dana. She was saying something about grass blades.

"Uh-huh," I said, trying to sound as intelligent as I knew how. Grass blades have never been one of my favorite subjects, though I do enjoy them after a heavy meal.

"From the way the grass was flattened, it's clear she was carried all the way from the tree to the pond and then dumped in."

She was moving at a good pace and I had to make an

effort to keep up. One of the disadvantages of being big is that it takes more energy to move from point A to point B. Something to do with an apple and a guy called Newton. "Dumped in?" I repeated, panting a little.

"Just like Lucy Knicx," she said. "Too bad the witness didn't have the nerve to stay the killer's hand."

"Your crew wasn't in place, then?" I said, as innocently as possible.

She gave me a bemused frown. "Crew? What crew?"

"Those heavies I saw before," I said. When she looked at me as if I was speaking dog, I elaborated. "Three ugly-looking and very unfriendly Peterbalds?"

"I don't know what you're talking about," she said finally. "I canvased the scene all by myself, though Frank dropped by later on to see if there was anything he could do."

Now it was my turn to frown. "But I thought…"

"The FSA is a very small organization, Tom. And I can assure you no Peterbalds have ever been signed to join. Which is not to say I have anything against Peterbalds," she quickly added, probably remembering some non-discrimination clause in the FSA statutes. Her next words confirmed this. "All cats are created equal after all."

I hesitated.

"Don't you agree?" she said, a little too vehemently for my taste. It was clearly a subject on which she held strong views.

"Oh, of course," I said, dispelling her fear that I was some sort of feline racist. "It's just that I did see three Peterbalds who were on their way to the elm tree last night. So I naturally assumed…"

"Yes, I see," she said, mulling over these words. "I wonder what they were doing there."

"You didn't see them?"

"No, though I did have the distinct impression I was

being watched at some point." She shrugged. "Probably just tourists."

"Yeah," I said, not convinced. Hadn't Brutus mentioned he'd seen Dana hobnobbing with the ugly trio? For a brief moment I toyed with the idea of confronting her with the truth, but then I dropped it. If there's one thing any secret agent worth his or her salt knows how to do with practiced ease, it's lying. There was no way I would get her to tell me the truth if she didn't want to. I had to try another tack. "Brutus said he thought they were from Southridge," I said.

"Oh?"

"Yeah, he said Southridgeans are swarming all over Brookridge trying to steal our natural resources."

"Is that so?" she said, uninterested.

"Especially our queens," I said, emphasizing the last word.

Dana simply ignored me. I gave it one last try.

"He said Southridgeans are probably behind these murders as well."

Dana looked up sharply. "Brutus is a silly ass and you can tell him so when you see him next."

"Oh-kay," I said, taken aback by this sudden snappishness.

"And what's all this talk about Brutus anyway?" she continued. "I thought you two didn't get along?"

"Well, it's like this…" I began, but she interrupted me.

"You'd better stay away from that cat," she said, fixing me with a fierce stare. "He's not good company for an FSA agent."

In my opinion Brutus wasn't good company for any cat, but I remained quiet, wondering what had brought on this sudden outburst.

"He's a meddling fool and the worst gossipmonger in all of Brookridge. That's why I often use him to spread a rumor. Within 24 hours every single cat roaming the Brookridge streets is briefed when Brutus gets a whiff of the story."

I knew all that, of course, but what I didn't know was why the mere mention of Southridgean involvement in Dana's murder investigation was enough to make her fly off the handle. If I didn't know any better I'd have said Brutus and Dana were... No way! "You and Brutus?" I exclaimed, a little too loudly.

"Shh!" Dana admonished me. We had just entered the Brookridge Park but she kept looking around as if the bushes had ears. "Not so loud!"

"Don't tell me you and Brutus are an item?" I said. But the way her face flushed told me enough. "Nooo..." I said, truly flabbergasted and appalled.

She finally fessed up. "Yes," she said with bowed head. "One summer, three years ago, Brutus and I had a brief..." Her voice trailed off.

"Oh, my God..." I said.

So there you go. Even a secret agent of Dana's obvious merit has deep, dark secrets hidden in her murky past. Shocking? Obviously. Surprising? Hardly. It merely confirms my theory that girls will fall for the muscular male, even if he's a mean, bullying dumb-ass like Brutus. But then again, I shouldn't speak badly of the brute. He is, after all, my newfound partner.

24

THE PIMPLED PUSTULE STRIKES
AGAIN

Though I was more than a little curious to know how a girl of Dana's obvious intelligence and attractiveness could ever fall for a guy like Brutus, it was clear she wasn't ready to discuss the affair, so I let it go. But between Dana's lies about the Peterbald triplets and her romantic liaison with Brookridge's gift to brutishness, it was safe to say that the plot was thickening.

We had arrived at the Brookridge Park pond, and I became aware of strange goings-on. The ducks were uncharacteristically quiet and a small band of humans had gathered on the other side from where we stood. I squinted to figure out what they were doing, and then it became clear: a lifeless body was resting on the patch of grass lining the pond and the men all stood hovering over it, frowning, and brooding.

"Jamie Burrow?" I said, and Dana nodded. She seemed suddenly distracted. Perhaps being reminded of her past love had brought back memories of happier days? I refrained from probing into the matter, and suggested we move in for a closer look. Humans never take much notice of cats anyway, so we could easily take a peek at the remains of unfortunate Jamie and perhaps learn something about the circumstances of her demise.

But oddly enough Dana seemed unwilling to proceed. She shook her head and said, in a small voice, "You go."

"But—"

"I-I can't."

So I shrugged and left her there while I hobbled to the other side of the pond. As luck would have it, a tree branch hung low over the scene and within seconds I was on it, enjoying a bird's eye view of the proceedings. Bart Ganglion was there, of course, a burly copper with a bristly mustache, as was Mayor Solomon McCrady, a fat little man who likes to think he's the most important man in all of Brookridge, which he probably is.

Stretched out on a piece of pea-green tarp was a smallish female human who may or may not have been pretty when alive but now looked positively unhealthy. Being dead does nothing for one's complexion. Hers was a pasty white, all color drained from her face. I gulped at the sight. Though it was the first time I'd laid eyes on this particular human, I felt sorry for Jamie Burrow. She was young and, before meeting the grim reaper, probably full of life, and didn't deserve to be chucked into the Brookridge Park pond as if she were duck food.

At this moment a smallish man with a horrid combover was examining the body with the air of the expert. The medical man, no doubt. Seeing him reminded me of the last time Zack had taken me to the vet. Syringes had played a huge part in the encounter and there had been a lot of talk about parasites and—oh, the horror—worms.

The memory somehow drew me closer to the recently departed, and I tried my darndest to pick up any hints or clues as to the identity of the vicious murderer who had slain young Jamie. Unfortunately, the men up top, or rather down below, were remarkably reticent about first causes, their discussion restricting itself to idle speculation on European soccer prognostics. Bart Ganglion seemed to think AC Milan would prevail in the Champions League, while the doctor had it on good authority that Manchester United was in excellent fettle and would lead the pack.

Then my eye fell on Frank, who was sitting by his master's side, and I tried to catch his eye by letting out a soft mewl. The white Poodle responded with satisfying alacrity by pricking up his ears and trying to pinpoint the source of my feline cry. It took two more yowls for him to figure out he needed to search the skies, not the earth, but then he finally caught on. After a curt nod, he ambled away towards the foot of the tree and I descended from my high perch to join him there.

25

CONVERSATIONS WITH DOGS

"And? What have you found out?" I said, dispensing with the customary pleasantries.

"If I had any money, I'd put my little all on Manchester United," Frank said, flicking his fluffy white tail excitedly.

"About the murder, you lummox," I said with some exasperation. I've never been able to understand this obsession with soccer and probably never will.

"Oh, that," he said, directing his gaze at Jamie's remains. "Seems she was stabbed in the back and then dumped in the pond."

"I know that," I said, wondering, not for the first time, how Frank had ever managed to become Brookridge's premier police dog. "What about the killer? Whodunit?"

He shrugged and scratched his ear with his hind leg. "Beats me. From the looks of it probably the same perp who did the Knicx girl."

"The pimpled pustule," I said.

"All evidence seems to point that way," he said.

"You don't seem to be overly concerned," I remarked, surprised that Frank, usually the first one to get all hot and bothered about any crime, whether it be public urination or some domestic disturbance between a tom and a queen, responded so tepidly.

"Oh, well," he said. "Bart has a pretty good idea who's behind all this." He then looked left and right to make sure we weren't being overheard, and leaned in. "Someone from Southridge, apparently."

"What's with all the Southridge bashing?" I said, annoyed that even Frank would go in for this small-mindedness.

"Why, you think it's a Brookridgean who's killing these women?" He shook his head decidedly, his ears flapping as he did so. "No way it's a local. You, for one, should know that."

"What's that supposed to mean?"

"Didn't you say you didn't recognize the killer when you saw him?"

"So?"

"So, if he was a Brookridgean you would have known him, right?"

This was extremely specious reasoning on his part, and I said as much. "You can hardly expect me to know every single person in Brookridge, now can you?"

"Still. I'm pretty sure our pimpled pervert is not from around here. Call it a hunch."

There. This is exactly the reason I never argue with a dog. When push comes to shove, they will always pull the instinct card, and then where are you? Cats never do that. They'll never make a wild guess and then try to blame their gut. But dogs? Every single time. "I won't call it a hunch, I'll call it bullsh—"

"Careful, Tom," said Frank, giving me the stern gaze. "You don't want to be arrested for insulting a police officer, do you?"

"But you're not a police officer!" I cried. "You're not even a police dog!"

He scraped the dirt with his paw and said, rather huffily I thought, "That's neither here nor there. Bart is a policeman. I'm Bart's dog. Ergo: I'm a police dog."

See? You simply can't argue with a canine. "Whatever," I said therefore, and decided to let the matter rest. If Frank wanted to believe the pimpled killer was a Southridgean, so be it. What it amounted to was that no one had a clue, and once again it was up to the FSA to figure out what was going on here.

"Have you seen Dana?" said Frank, scraping the ground with his other paw. And for the first time I noticed a hint of animation in his voice.

"Dana? Sure, she's right over there," I said, pointing to where I'd left my senior officer.

This bit of intel had an instant effect on Frank: his head shot up, his tail stretched out, and for a moment he gave a very good impression of a pointing dog.

I frowned, this type of behavior reminding me of something, but what... Then it struck me. Zack always acts this way when he's under the influence of one of his infatuations.

"Don't tell me you're..."

Frank jerked his head around. "What?" he said, a little bit too defensively for my taste.

"In love with Dana?" I said, incredulous.

"Don't be ridiculous," he huffed. "Who has ever heard of a dog falling in love with a cat? It's simply not done." He swallowed, and suddenly the same type of hangdog look came over him that I've also noticed with Zack. Though it looked better on Frank, he actually being a dog, I mean.

"You've got it bad, haven't you?" I said in my best bedside voice.

He simply nodded, looking miserable.

This explained why he seemed less than interested in the

mystery of the pimpled killer all of a sudden. Spurned love will do that to a man. Or, in this case, a dog.

"What? She doesn't like you? Is that it?"

He heaved a deep sigh, and shook his head dejectedly. "I haven't even told her yet." He suddenly looked up and directed a fierce look in my direction. "And don't you go blabbing about it, Tom. I want to be the one to tell her."

"Well, then tell her," I said simply. I've never understood why males in love will make these things so overly complicated. If you're in love with a gal, just go over and tell her. If she likes you, she'll giggle. And if she doesn't, she'll, well, also giggle. No giggle has ever killed a man. Or dog. Or cat.

"But I can't tell her," he wailed. "I'm a dog. She's a cat. It's not right. It's not... natural. What if we have kids? What will they look like? Half canine, half feline?"

"I wouldn't worry too much if I were you," I said. "For one thing, chances are that Dana doesn't even like you." A sudden howl of anguish told me this wasn't the right avenue to pursue. "Or, perhaps she does," I amended. Remembering how hesitant Dana was to join me at the crime scene, I started to see her reluctance had more to do with the fact that Frank was there than with a sudden aversion to the sight of dead bodies.

"What should I do?" he cried, and I now saw that the humans were starting to take notice of Frank's yowls.

"Look, why don't I talk to Dana about your, um..." I began.

"No! Not a word!"

"But—"

"Not a word to Dana, Tom! Promise me!"

I rolled my eyes. "Oh, all right," I said. "Be that way if you must. But I have a pretty strong suspicion the feeling is mutual."

His eyes lit up at this piece of news. "Y-y-you think so?"

I nodded emphatically. "Trust me. I know about these things."

"I forgot about that," he said.

The entire feline and canine population of Brookridge is probably aware of Zack's infatuation problem by now, as I've regaled pretty much everyone with my fount of funny Zack-stories.

"So, as the resident expert on love and romance..."

He hesitated, drawing a heart in the soil with first his left, then his right paw. Finally he relented. "You can tell her. But be discrete, will you, Tom?"

"Sure. Call me Mister Discretion."

For some odd reason, he didn't seem convinced.

KILLER OF THE YEAR

Frank's words had left a deep impression on me. No, not the bit about harboring feelings stronger than mere friendship for La Dana, though this revelation of inter-species love had surprised me. What had made me think a bit was the fact that everyone seemed to assume that the killer hailed from Southridge, simply because both Dana and I had failed to identify him.

Now, though it's true I know my fair share of Brookridgeans, and so does Dana, it's stretching the boundaries of our networking capabilities to suppose that we know every single person who lives within the town borders. It's probably safe to say I know everyone who lives around Main Street and the Market Square, as well as Tulip Street, Bellflower Street and Geranium Street. But beyond that...

I'd reached the place where I'd last seen Dana, and found to my surprise that she wasn't there. I'm sorry to say that the first thing that went through my mind was that she must have met up with Brutus and that the two of them were taking a romantic stroll through the park, rekindling the old feelings. I shivered at the thought of Dana linking her lot to

Brutus, and directed my step towards the elm tree where it had all began. Perhaps she was waiting for me there.

It's one of those inconveniences of being a cat; we don't carry around cell phones—and even if we did, I wouldn't know where to put it, as I've never worn pants and I very much doubt I ever will. If I'd had a cell phone, I could have simply rung up Dana and dispensed with all this searching here, there and everywhere. For she wasn't at the elm tree, and neither was she to be found at the bandstand, the miniature golf course or the playground.

And it was as I was trudging along in the direction of the amphitheater Mayor McCrady had opened with much fanfare just the month before, that I had the shock of a lifetime. Walking along the path, pushing a pram, a little girl of about four clinging to his hand, was the pimpled killer! I gasped, I reeled, I swayed, but after a second, third and fourth look, he was still there, cool as a cucumber and heading my way. The pimple was losing its plumpness, but the rest of his face was just the way I'd remembered. Broad and pasty, with a smattering of pockmarks along the rim, and two dark eyes taking in the sights from under drooping eyelids.

I wanted to scream and shout, but of course did nothing of the kind. I know what vicious killers do to witnesses, and even though I was merely a cat, I wasn't so sure he'd make an exception for me. And seeing as I was alone and in no position to warn my FSA compadres, I decided to tail the perp and find out who he was and where he lived.

My heart was pounding in my throat, my breathing had become stertorous, and I had trouble walking a straight line as my limbs were quaking with every step, but I was resolved to see this through. I'd identify the Brookridge Park killer and see justice served or my name wasn't Agent Tom. Visions of celebratory ceremonies and my name writ large in the

FSA annals drifted before my mind's eye as I stayed low and out of sight and waddled after the pimpled killer.

The shock of seeing the man abating a little, I now started to wonder what he was doing here, and what was more, why he was accompanied by a small child and what I assumed to be a baby. I don't have a lot of firsthand experience dealing with killers, only knowing the breed from television cop shows, but they usually don't strike me as the fatherly type.

Still staying in the bushes lining the path, I watched with surprise as the killer set off for an ice cream stall and proceeded to treat the little girl to an ice cream cone and buy one for himself, as well. The girl was obviously pleased, beaming up at the man and planting a big, wet kiss on his cheek.

"Thank you, daddy!" she exclaimed, and I blinked.

Daddy? For a moment there I'd assumed the guy to be a kidnapper. These being tough economic times, taking a second job wasn't all that uncommon, and I'm not sure there's a lot of money in being a murdering maniac. But if my ears hadn't deceived me—and they seldom did—the girl was his... daughter?

The girl now leaned over the pram and dropped a small dollop of ice cream into its interior. A mirthful gurgle confirmed the treat was well received by the pram's inhabitant, clearly some human infant. All the while, the pimpled killer was looking on with a look of such fatherly devotion written all over his pasty face, that I had a hard time keeping in mind this man was indeed the Brookridge Park butcher.

Of course, as I've indicated, my life hitherto has been pretty much killer-free, so the rules and regulations governing this particular type of human are unfamiliar to me. Perhaps all killers are devoted parents? Perhaps they all dote on their offspring the way this specimen did?

I watched with fascination, therefore, and not a little bit

of fearful exhilaration, as I continued to track the man's progression along the park's lanes. He now parked himself and his little girl on a bench alongside the pond and I saw to my horror that on the other side of the pond a Red Cross vehicle had drawn up and two burly nurses were transferring Jamie Burrow's remains onto a stretcher of sorts.

This was getting too weird: the killer looking on as his latest victim was being removed from the scene. I had taken up vigil in the bush closest to the bench and was studying the man's face as he watched the proceedings. More than a mild interest didn't seem to stir his features, the kind of curiosity that drives rubberneckers and thrill seekers to gather round the scene of a car crash.

"What are those people doing over there, daddy?" said the girl, having managed to deposit more ice cream on her shirt-front than in her stomach.

"That's an ambulance, honey," said the man, unperturbed.

The girl seemed to know what an ambulance was, for she said, "Is one of the ducks sick, daddy?"

The man chuckled. "I don't think so. Probably someone was not feeling well. It happens a lot when it's as warm as today."

"I know what happened," said the girl, nodding sagely. "Someone forgot to eat their ice cream and got too hot." She then looked from her own half-melted, half-eaten cone to the ambulance. "Should I give them mine, daddy?"

"That's all right, honey. I don't think eating your ice cream will make them feel better. When people get sick, ice cream is not what they want."

The girl's face lit up. "They need apsirin!"

"Aspirin," corrected her father.

"That's what I said," said the girl, sploshing more ice cream on her shirt.

The scene puzzled me. This guy didn't look like a killer to

me. I studied his nose and its most distinguishing feature: the pimple. Yes, it was the same fellow, I was sure of it. I sighed as it started to dawn on me that the life of the feline spy is not an easy one. Just when you think you've got the murder investigation all wrapped up in a neat bundle, your killer goes and turns out to be father of the year.

27

INTERSPECIES MINGLING

From the corner of my eye I detected movement and, turning around without letting the killer out of my sight, I saw that it was Dana. She snuck up next to me and heaved, "What's going on?"

She appeared out of breath. "Where have you been?" I said, with not a little bit of pique, for I hadn't forgotten how she had walked out on me.

But Dana gasped as her eye fell on the pasty-faced father of two. "That's the killer!" she exclaimed. "You've found him!"

She directed an admiring look at me that mollified me to a great extent. "Just happened to bump into him," I said modestly. "How did you find me, by the way?"

"I tracked your frequency," she said, as if it was the most obvious thing in the world. She pointed at the girl. "Who's the kid?"

"You won't believe this," I said, "but our killer is a devoted family man." And I proceeded to regale her with a blow-by-blow account of my detection work up to that point. She whistled through her teeth, something I'd never seen any cat do before, not even Brutus.

"It doesn't add up," she said, studying the man's face. She nodded slowly. "It is the same guy, I'm sure of it."

"So am I," I said.

"It's not just his face. I can sense his frequency, and it reads the same as the killer's."

"Couldn't you have tracked him down by his frequency, then? Like you did with me?"

She grimaced. "I tried that, but couldn't draw a bead on him. It was almost as if his frequency was jammed or something. Though I can't even begin to imagine how that is possible."

"The plot thickens," I said ominously.

"It does indeed," Dana said.

For a moment we stared at our killer in silence, as he wiped his little girl's face with a napkin, the image of the loving father.

"That reminds me," I said. "You have a secret admirer."

"Oh?" She didn't seem surprised. Cats like Dana collect secret, and not so secret, admirers by the boatload.

I was pretty sure she'd already read my mind, but I said it, anyway. One likes to cherish these old-fashioned habits. "Frank the Poodle has professed his undying love and devotion to you." And if that wasn't a discrete way of putting it, I didn't know what was.

A smile lit up her furry face. "I know. That's why I didn't want to join you before. I didn't want to embarrass Frank. He *will* get all goofy when he sees me."

"I thought as much."

It is hard to detect a blush in an animal so royally decorated with fur as a cat, but I had the distinct impression a blush was actually creeping up Dana's cheeks at this very moment. "My God!" I exclaimed. "You feel the same way about him, don't you?"

She nodded bashfully, probably the first time I'd ever seen

Dana display any form of demureness. She sighed a happy sigh. "I do," she finally said.

"But—but—but—"

She raised her eyes. "I know. He's a dog and I'm a cat and interspecies mingling is unnatural and yadda yadda yadda. Spare me the platitudes. I've heard them all before. The simple fact of the matter is that I'm in love and I don't care who knows it."

"No one knows it," I interjected.

"I know. And I would very much like to keep it that way. So, not a word to anyone, you hear me, Tom?"

I blinked. Hadn't she just told me she was in love and didn't care who knew? "I, erm…"

"Not even to Frank. I don't want him to hear it from anyone but me that I…" She smiled. "Love the hell out of that big, fluffy Poodle."

I gave her my solemn word that my lips were sealed, and then reminded her there were more pressing matters to be dealt with right now. Like, bringing the Brookridge Park killer to justice.

For a moment, she seemed reluctant to drop the discussion of her love life, but then she shelved the topic and focused on the matter at hand. "I think the best avenue to pursue is to talk to Frank," she said.

"Forget about Frank," I urged. "I'm sure he'll make you a swell partner but solving Lucy and Jamie's murders is more important right now."

She eyed me critically. "Are you quite finished? We need Frank to transfer the murderer's identity to Bart, so that he can make an arrest."

"Oh," I said.

"Oh, indeed. Now all I need right now is to know this guy's name and—"

"Can't you just, you know, scan it? Get into his mind?"

"No, I can't. I don't know how many times a day you think about your own name..."

Quite often, in fact, I wanted to say, but I kept my mouth shut. One doesn't like to come across as a narcissist.

"I thought so," she said, as she read my mind. "But most people don't. Oh, I'm sure we could find out his name eventually, if we follow him around long enough, but if this guy really is a serial killer, it's imperative we get him into police custody as soon as possible. So the best thing to do is for you to steal his wallet."

There was a lot to be said about this modus operandi, but I refrained from saying it, for our killer decided this was the moment to start moving again.

28

THE BELLE OF THE BALL

J'd never been involved in the pursuit of a vicious killer before, and certainly not one that demanded I somehow obtain the latter's wallet. I was wracking my brain how to accomplish this seemingly impossible task, when a bit of luck had Stevie cross our path. Killer and family had just exited the park and had taken a left toward the Brookridge Market Square, when I saw Stevie ambling up. He raised a paw in greeting and I waved him over.

"Howdy," he said good-naturedly. "How's my FSA crew today?"

"Don't mention that word," hissed Dana.

"Be quiet," I hissed.

"What's going on?" whispered Stevie, for he could put two and two together just like the next cat.

"See that guy over there?" I said, pointing at our friendly neighborhood killer.

"Is that…" he said, squinting.

Both Dana and I nodded emphatically.

"He doesn't look like much of a killer," said Stevie, sounding disappointed. "More like an accountant."

"Those are usually the worst," I said, for lack of anything else to say.

"Hey, I finally induced Sam to dream up the meaning of that word you were looking for. Um…" He paused, pondering.

"Bluebell?" I ventured.

He pointed a nicely buffed claw at me. "Bingo. I sat next to the man all night. You wouldn't believe what kind of stuff he dreams about."

"I can," I said. "I was there, remember?"

"Right. I forgot." He then turned his attention to Dana. "And how's my favorite secret agent this fine morning?" he said.

"Stevie!" I said.

"Huh?"

I gave him my most exasperated look. "Bluebell?"

"Oh, of course. Bluebell. Well, turns out Bluebell is in fact—"

"What's Bluebell?" interrupted Dana.

All this time we'd been trailing Killer & family from afar, and the tension of trying to keep up with him and at the same time inducing Stevie to divulge the information he'd culled from Father Sam's dreams, was weighing on me. So much so that I'd temporarily forgotten all about my newly acquired mind-reading capabilities.

Now remembering I didn't have to wait for Stevie to get his facts straight but could simply take a peek inside his noggin, I did so. And came up with nothing. Odd, I felt. Either Stevie's mind was a complete blank, or else I'd lost my new powers overnight. I tried again and again drew a blank.

I then tried to read Dana's mind and, once again, came away with zilch. Extremely frustrating. Oh, well, I thought. Probably these new skills take some time to settle. And I decided to try again a little later.

In the meantime, Stevie had brought Dana up to date on the whole Bluebell mystery and she, too, was now burning with anticipation to learn more.

"Bluebell is…" Stevie said, then paused for effect.

"What? What?" I said, barely suppressing an exasperated groan.

"Well, Bluebell isn't Bluebell at all."

"Stevie!" I said.

"But it isn't!" he said. "All this time we thought it was the name of a girl, but in fact it's the description of a character in the play. Blue belle is the name Sam uses to describe the murder victim in Murder in the Park. In other words, Zoe Huckleberry."

He gave us the look a magician gives at the end of a particularly startling performance. All that was missing was 'ta-dah!'

"One of the key scenes in the play is a big ball at some castle somewhere," Stevie continued, "at the end of which Zoe Huckleberry is killed in the castle park by her lover Jack Mackintosh after he finds out she's been cheating on him with his best friend, who turns out to have set the whole thing up to get rid of Zoe as a way to get back at Zoe's husband, a well-known and highly respectable gynecologist, whom he holds responsible for the death of his wife, who died in childbirth some twenty-odd years before."

He paused for breath. Dana and I merely goggled, trying to follow the narrative. I don't read mystery stories as a rule, so hearing the plotline of one described in a single sentence had my mind reeling for a spell.

"And since Zoe Huckleberry wears a blue dress to the ball and is described by any and all as the belle of the ball, she's referred to by director and acting troupe as the blue belle."

So that's why there was no reference to Bluebell in the

script. It wasn't an official name but merely a nickname thought up by Sam to describe one of the characters.

"So Lucy Knicx was the blue belle until she was murdered," said Stevie. "Then Jamie Burrow held the title for a while, and now…"

"Don't tell me they've appointed someone else to play the part," said Dana, aghast.

Stevie nodded solemnly. "You won't like this, Dana. It's Barbara."

"Barbara? Which Barbara?" said Dana, swallowing.

"Your Barbara," said Stevie. "Since they ran out of understudies, Barbara volunteered for the part. She's the new blue belle."

"Oh, no," groaned Dana.

"Oh, yes," said Stevie. "And apparently she's already told all of Brookridge about her starring role, as she likes to call it."

I think I've mentioned before that Barbara Vale, Dana's human and secretary to the Mayor's secretary Fisk Grackle, is one of the more prominent gossipmongers in all of Brookridge. It is said that her tongue works faster than a sewing machine, but I'm sure that's just nasty gossip.

"But the premiere is tonight!"

Both Stevie and I exchanged worried glances. It's one thing for any ordinary human to get stabbed to death, but when it's one of *our* humans, it's a different matter altogether.

We were still trailing our serial killer, and it now became obvious there was some urgency in bringing him to justice. We still didn't know why this man was so keen on killing off every 'blue belle' scheduled to appear in the Theatrical Society's performance of Murder in the Park, but it was paramount that he be stopped.

I was still desperately trying to come up with some way

of stealing the man's wallet, when a bit of luck came our way. Our target, who had been sauntering along, enjoying the sun and a stroll with his family, was now hailed by a passerby.

"Hey, Norbert!" said the passerby, a gray-haired plump sort of bird. "How's tricks?"

A long and utterly boring conversation ensued, but Dana, Stevie and I didn't hang around to follow it to its conclusion. We had a first name, and that was enough. There probably weren't all that many Jack Mackintosh understudies going around answering to the name Norbert, so as far as the FSA was concerned, our work here was done. Next stop: Frank the Poodle.

29

BRING IN THE CONSTABULARY

*D*ana chose not to join our tryst with Brookridge's canine finest, and when we had finally located the sniffing sleuth, Frank seemed oddly out of sorts.

"Hullo," he barked moodily.

Per Dana's instructions, we had tracked the police dog down at the police station, where he liked to keep officer Bart Ganglion company of a morning. We had found him lying at Bart's feet with his head on his front paws, staring gloomily into space, and had attracted his attention by softly mewling from the police station's window, which had been left ajar.

Pricking up his dangling fluffy ears, he slowly raised his eyebrows to take us in, and, very reluctantly, rose to his paws and ambled over to where we sat for a tête-à-tête.

"Hullo," he barked once again in that voice from the tomb.

"Frankie," said Stevie cheerily. "How's it hanging, dog?"

Frank gave Stevie a scornful look, but didn't deign to respond.

"The little lady let you down?" continued Stevie, who doesn't have a sensitive bone in his body.

Frank frowned. "What do you know about my little lady?" he said suspiciously. He then directed an accusing glance at me. 'Have you been blabbing?' it seemed to say.

I merely shook my head to indicate my innocence.

"Oh, my God!" exclaimed Stevie suddenly, his eyes widening. "You and Dana? You're an item?"

I closed my eyes. What I'd forgotten was that Stevie could now read minds, and Frank's mind was brimming with but a single thought: Dana. I could have put Frank out of his misery by bringing him the good news that the lady he loved, loved him, but decided against it. I'd given Dana my word, and my word is my bond. At least when given to cats like Dana, whom I pretty sure can kill man or beast with a single glance.

"Look, we really don't have time to go into all of that," I said. "We've got more important matters to deal with right now."

As indeed we had. When there're killers on the loose, the local policeman's dog's romantic predilections are the last thing one wants to discuss.

Stevie gazed at me with accusing eyes. "What? You knew about this? And you didn't tell me? Me? Your partner?"

"I was sworn to secrecy, all right?" I said a little impatiently. All this talk about Dana and Frank was starting to annoy me. What was the big deal, anyway? Love knows no bounds. And even though I'd never personally experienced the big L yet, I heartily agreed with the pairing. Dana, though highly strung, was a swell girl, and Frank, though an oaf, a swell guy.

"I thought we secret agents had no secrets from one another?" Stevie said, his red whiskers twitching. It was obvious my reticence had touched him deeply.

"It's no big deal," I said.

"It is to me," he said. "I tell you all *my* secrets."

"You have no secrets, Stevie," I said, exasperated.

"I do, too," he said huffily. "I've got plenty."

But before he could start listing them, Frank interrupted. "Is there a reason for this visit? Or did you merely come to annoy me?" He spoke rather gruffly, I thought. Which was probably understandable, under the circumstances. No ardent lover likes a critic.

"We found out who killed Lucy Knicx and Jamie Burrow," I said quickly, cutting off Stevie, who had just opened his mouth to complain some more.

This had Frank perk up visibly. "Who is it?" he said, looking from me to Stevie.

"All we know is that he's called Norbert, that he's an understudy for the part of Jack Mackintosh in the Murder in the Park play, and that he's got two kids, one of whom likes ice cream." And I proceeded to give Frank a brief account of our fact-finding mission.

"That must be Norbert McIlroy," he said pensively.

"Is he from Southridge?" I said, wanting to put Brutus's theory to the test.

Frank shook his head, his ears dangling to and fro. "He lives in the Friar Tuck Street," he said. "On the other side of town."

"So, now you go do your thing," said Stevie, "and we can all rest easier, knowing that a vicious killer is safely behind bars."

Since neither Stevie nor I qualified for the role of Zoe Huckleberry, I didn't think we had much to fear from Norbert McIlroy's murderous instincts, but Stevie was right. Brookridge would be a better, finer place without the likes of Norbert roaming the streets at night, his big, shiny knife at the ready.

Frank wasn't convinced. "I'm not convinced," he said. "For one thing, Norbert doesn't have any priors."

"What's a prior?" said Stevie.

I could have told him, for Zack and I like to watch our cop show of an evening, but I let Frank do the honors.

"Prior arrests or convictions," man's most loyal friend elucidated. "Norbert's rap sheet is squeaky clean."

"What's a rap sheet?" said Stevie.

"It means that Norbert doesn't have a criminal record," I said.

"So what?" said Stevie. "Perhaps he was never caught before. Or else he only now discovered murder agrees with him. Some people are like that. Takes them ages to figure out where their talents lie. Take Father Sam for instance. No one would have thought he had it in him to be a director. And yet he is. And doing a damn fine job of it, as well. Not a day goes buy without some ingénue knocking on his door wanting his expert opinion on her performance. Lucy Knicx did. And so did Jamie Burrow."

Stevie had a point there, but Frank didn't buy it. "Norbert is a gentle soul," he said. "He wouldn't hurt a fly."

"He doesn't have to hurt flies," said Stevie. "We're not talking about flies here. We're talking about women. Don't muddle the conversation with these false arguments, Frank."

"What I mean," said Frank, annoyed, "is that Norbert is a family man and one of Brookridge's most upstanding citizens."

"What does he do for a living?" I said.

Frank hesitated. "He's a butcher," he finally said.

"Ha!" said Stevie. "I knew it!"

"Just whisper Norbert's name in Bart's ear, Frank," I urged. "He'll bring him in for questioning and then we'll see what happens. I'm sure he has fingerprints or DNA or whatever, that could link Norbert to the crime."

"And two eye witnesses," added Stevie. "One of whom is your sweetheart."

Frank drew himself up to his full height at these words, and I felt it imperative I speak the soothing word. "I don't think the testimony of two cats is admissible in court, Stevie," I said.

"Why not?" said Stevie. "Our word is as good as a human's."

"For one thing, cats don't talk human," I said, throwing a nervous glance at Frank, who still sat glowering at Stevie.

Stevie conceded I had a point there. "Though I think it's discrimination, pure and simple," he said.

"What's discrimination is that police dogs aren't allowed to murder members of the citizenry," growled Frank, clenching and unclenching his paws.

30

SECOND UNDERSTUDY TO THE RESCUE

*A*s I left the police station, I was musing on the curious transformation that had come over my part-ner, Stevie. The Ragamuffin had always struck me as some-thing of a goofball. Not too smart, but basically good-hearted and sweet. Throughout our recent encounter with Frank, though, Stevie had been downright mean to the police dog. So much so that I started to wonder if his recent entry into the FSA ranks had something to do with this. Perhaps becoming a secret agent had gone to Stevie's head?

Deciding to have a word with Dana about this, I returned home. I wasn't used to staying up until all hours of the day, and I felt an urgent desire to take a long and refreshing nap. Slipping in through the cat door, I headed straight for the couch. The moment my belly hit the pillow, I was lost to the world and all of its qualms.

I woke up to the sound of snoring somewhere in my vicinity, and, lifting my head, I saw that Zack had joined me on the couch and was sleeping like a log. Zack is the kind of person who easily gets tired of working the same job, so he likes to change things around from time to time. In other words, he's one of those jack of all trades and master of none types of guys. Currently, he's between jobs, so he spends a lot of time at home catching up on his sleep and reruns of Columbo, Murder She Wrote and Castle, his favorite shows.

I ambled over to my human, curled up in his lap, and nodded off again. The sound of the phone ringing off the hook made us both sit up with a jerk. Rubbing the sleep from his eyes, Zack stumbled into the hallway to pick up the phone and I stretched the last remnants of sleep from my limbs. I was pretty sure that Frank had done his police dog's duty, Bart his policeman's duty, the magistrate his legal duty, and that Norbert McIlroy was now residing safely behind lock and key. All my troubles, in other words, were over.

Unfortunately, I couldn't have been more wrong.

Zack, returning the receiver to its cradle, rubbed his chin thoughtfully, and, reading his mind, I could see why. He'd been talking to Father Sam on the phone. Due to unforeseen circumstances, Norbert McIlroy had dropped out of the play, and Zack had been promoted to play the part of Jack Mackintosh in Murder in the Park. Far from being ecstatic, though, Zack was clearly unhappy.

Muttering something under his breath, he retreated into the kitchen and started rifling through the wastepaper basket. Retrieving a torn and tattered pile of papers, he proceeded to smooth out the mess, and took a seat at the kitchen table, the Murder in the Park script—for that was what it was—in front of him.

Listlessly thumbing through its pages, he sighed as he took in the passages marked in yellow. Once upon a time he'd been keen on appearing in the play, and had even started cramming the Jack Mackintosh lines. Then, when it became clear to him that the second understudy has about zilch chance of actually getting any stage time, he'd simply chucked the play and forgotten all about it.

Now being informed by Father Sam that he was due to walk on stage in just a few hours, he wasn't too keen on trying to memorize the part after all. And then there was the fact that Sam had informed him that he was supposed to kiss Barbara Vale, who was now playing the blue belle part. Zack groaned as he read the first Mackintosh line aloud.

"Oh, my darling, darling love."

I couldn't blame him. Locking lips with either Lucy Knicx or Jamie Burrow had clearly appealed to Zack a lot more than the prospect of clasping Mrs. Vale to his bosom. One didn't even have to be a mind reader to interpret the reason Zack was now pulling at the few remaining strands of hair on his head. The man was unhappy to a large degree.

"Oh, my sweet, sweet love…"

Unable to stomach the agony of a strong man faced with bad scriptwriting, I exited the scene center left. Throwing one last glance over my shoulder, I caught a glimpse of Zack taking a hefty butcher's knife out of the kitchen drawer, and brandishing it about in an underhand grip.

For some reason, the sight gave me the shivers, and I suddenly felt oddly apprehensive about Zack taking on the role of Jack Mackintosh. Why this was, I couldn't have said, but I suddenly wanted, more than anything, that he hadn't accepted the part.

MEETING PETER BALD

*A*s far as I was concerned, life was back to normal. So I strolled to the park as dusk started to fall, and made my way to my favorite elm tree to take up position in its welcoming arms. Many a season I now had passed in this tree, and its sturdy branches were my home away from home. Hopping deftly onto my high perch, I was reminded once again of the recent happenings that had rocked my world, so to speak, and wondered what the future would hold, now that I was an FSA agent.

I smiled as I closed my eyes. Since nothing ever happens in Brookridge, I had the distinct impression this whole FSA thing would simply go away. I sighed a happy sigh, and prepared to take my evening slumber when a voice grated on my nervous system.

"Hey, wart face!" spoke the voice.

I sat up as if stung, for I recognized its timbre.

"Answer me or die, carpetbag," the voice came.

Looking down, I perceived I once more had the pleasure of the Peterbalds' company. Or rather, Peterbald, for this time only one of the ugly heavies had shown up, ostensibly the leader of the pack.

"Are you addressing me?" I said with as much hauteur as I could muster while suppressing a tendency to shake from stem to stern.

"Who else, furball?" my visitor said in his gravelly voice. "Are you coming down or do I have to come up?"

"I'll come down," I said quickly, and had joined the Peterbald before he could come up with another insulting noun to describe my person.

The sinewy cat smirked at me, and I caught a glimpse of something stuck between his razor-sharp teeth. Whether it was a fishbone or a piece of splintered human skull I couldn't tell, but the sight made me wish the fellow would stop smiling.

"Nice weather we've been having, don't you think?" I said. To my annoyance my voice sounded shrill and reedy.

He eyed me malevolently but didn't speak, so I pushed on. "I just hope it will hold. According to the weatherman there's a storm front pushing in from the East, which might collide with the high pressure zone rolling in from the Azores."

"Are you just going to keep blabbing away like a fishmonger's wife, or are you going to shut up and listen?" he grunted.

"Shut up and listen," I said.

"Excellent choice." He glanced left and right and licked his lips. "Your boy Zack is going to murder the Vale woman tonight. And if I were you I'd make sure he doesn't."

"What? No! That's impossible. Zack would never do such a thing."

"And yet he will," he said slowly, giving me what I perceived was the evil eye.

"You're kidding, right?" I said, smiling my bravest smile. "A little joke?"

He looked at me levelly. "Do I look like I'm kidding?"

"Well, no," I admitted, shuffling uneasily. "But Zack would never murder anyone. He's not the murdering type."

"I never said he was. But he's still going to butcher the Vale if you don't put a stop to it."

"But—"

"You better leave now. The party's about to start and if you're not there, you won't have a home to return to tonight."

"But who are you? What's going on? Why would Zack do such a thing?"

He shook his head censoriously. "They told me you were a blabbermouth. Now get lost."

"What? No, I want—" I swallowed, blanching under the Peterbald's penetrating gaze. But still I persisted. "I want some answers," I said.

"You can ask me one question," the bald menace snarled.

"Who are you?" I said, before I could think things through. As it was, it was the question foremost in my mind.

He grinned, and worked the fishbone or human skull splinter loose with a yellow, pockmarked tongue, then transferred it to the other side of his maw. "Let's just say I work for the cat who runs the FSA. And now beat it, Agent Tom. You've got your orders. Now carry them out."

I suppressed a sudden urge to shout, 'Sir, yes, sir!' but merely nodded—intelligently, I hoped—and took my leave. I still had dozens of questions whirling through my mind, but refrained from voicing them. For one thing, where did this guy get all his information? And how could he be so sure? And, most of all, how could he think Zack—Zack of all people!—was even capable of such a thing?

But now was clearly not the time to go into first causes or sit down for a cozy one-on-one, so I simply ran as fast as my chubby legs could carry me to the Brookridge Market

Square, where the town theater is located. I had no idea how to stop what was about to unfold, nor how I would get close to the affair, as cats are not considered valued theatergoers, but I pushed on regardless.

What I did do was send out mental messages to Dana, Stevie and even Brutus, in the hope they would pick up on them and respond with alacrity to my silent cries for urgent assistance. I didn't know if this was the way to transmit a message, but I seemed to remember Dana saying something about picking up distress signals from other cats. And if she could pick up a signal from any Tom, Mitzi and Felix, she would surely pick one up from her FSA comrade. Or so I silently hoped.

AT THE THEATER

*A*rriving at the theater, I immediately proceeded to the back entrance, hoping to slip in through some crack, grate or open window. And I was just giving the building a once-over, trying to pinpoint its entrance possibilities, when my eyes met an uplifting sight: Dana came tripping down the alley in my direction, a worried expression on her face.

I gave an inward cheer. My mental projection, or whatever it was, had clearly worked. Then a loud bark came from behind her, and I saw that she wasn't alone: Frank had joined her and now came trotting up, looking a lot more cheerful than he had the last time we'd met. I didn't have to read his mind to come to the conclusion that Dana had told him the good news.

"What's going on?" said Dana, slightly out of breath. I now realized she was in fact a pretty pretty cat. Stomping on the thought—she was, after all, with Frank now—I quickly filled the both of them in on the state of affairs.

"Zack?" exclaimed Dana. "But that's impossible. We caught the killer."

"Bart locked up Norbert McIlroy this afternoon," grunted Frank. "Though he denies all charges."

"There's one other thing," I said. "This Peterbald I met said he works for the FSA."

Dana hesitated, then inclined her head. "He does. From your description it must be Dollo Rosso. He's the head of Internal Affairs."

"Internal Affairs?" I said, marveling at the intel. For one thing, I'd almost dismissed the FSA as a hoax of some kind, and now the organization turned out to have an Internal Affairs division. From my extensive research into Hollywood movies and TV shows I knew such a division mainly existed to subject its own members to extensive scrutiny, sniffing out any malfeasance on their part. I swallowed.

"They're investigating... me?" I said.

Dana shook her head. "No. They are not, at this time, investigating anyone in particular. IA branch reports directly to the FSA Director, who likes to keep a close eye on all of the organization's operations. For some reason this particular mission must have attracted his attention so he sent in Dollo Rosso and his crew."

"But how can they think Zack would ever..." I didn't finish the sentence, still thinking it beyond ludicrous they'd see a murderer in my human.

Dana had no answer to that. "All I know is that the Director's sources are impeccable, so there must be some truth to the matter."

The notion of hypnosis suddenly sprang to mind. The fact that Norbert, an upstanding citizen and father of two, denied all charges against his person indicated something fishy was going on. Perhaps someone had induced McIlroy to act the part of the murderer?

There have been cases of people committing an act of such atrocity the public cries foul, but later it turns out the perpetrator of such a crime was him-or herself an innocent victim of a third party, using mental or chemical stimulants to force the killer's hand. Could something like that be the case here? It certainly started to look like it.

I suggested this explanation to Dana and Frank, and they both agreed there might be something in it.

"But, if that's the case, then Norbert really *is* innocent," I said, "and the real killer is still on the loose."

"And now he's trying to do the same thing to Zack," said Frank.

"Whatever the explanation," said Dana, "we have to get in there, and stop your human from..." She swallowed. "... murdering my human."

In my consternation, I'd totally forgotten the predicament Barbara Vale was in. If Dollo Rosso was right, not one but two cats would lose their humans tonight. It was imperative we get inside and stop this drama from unfolding.

The three of us looked up at the back entrance to the theater. For a moment, I didn't see a way in. The entire building was painted black, probably out of some artistic consideration, and for a moment gave me the impression of one of those impregnable fortresses of old.

On the ground floor there was one entrance, marked Stage Door, and it featured a gangly youth standing watch. Then there was a garage of sorts, where I guess trucks with costumes and decors could back into, but that was closed now. On the first floor I noticed a window standing ajar, but there was no convenient drainpipe leading up to it and no other way of reaching it, so that was also a bust.

"We have got to get through that door," said Frank, pointing to the gangly kid. He looked about sixteen, with a dreadlocked goatee, an Evil Dead T-shirt, and iPod buds in his ears. His head was swaying to the rhythm of some beat, and he looked positively goofy to me. I had a feeling I'd seen him somewhere before, and then I remembered. He was one of Terrell McCrady's younger brothers.

"Isn't that Terris McCrady?" I said. I can never remember who is who in the McCrady household. There's four brothers—Terrell, Terrill, Terris and Terrence—and one girl —Terry—and they all look alike to me.

Frank nodded. "That's Terris all right. And I know just the thing to distract him." He coughed. "Better not watch this. It's not gonna be pretty."

I started. "You're not going to hurt him, are you?"

Frank grimaced. "Better turn away, Tom. You, too, Dana. Sensitive viewers, beware."

I swallowed a lump in my throat. I liked Terris. He'd once come to babysit me when Zack was away in England on some mission. I didn't like his choice of music—trance if I'm not mistaken—but no kid should be condemned for having bad taste. I averted my gaze as Frank moved in. The next moment horrible sounds echoed through the alley, and inadvertently I took a peek.

Frank the Poodle was lying on his back, four legs in the air, his tongue lolling, and producing puppy sounds, as Terris was tickling his belly.

"Now!" said Dana, and the both of us scooted out from our hiding place behind a dumpster, and raced to the stage door, which was now unguarded.

I looked back at Frank as I disappeared through the door. He caught my eye and I saluted him for the brave soldier that he was, laying his dignity on the line for the good of the mission.

We were in, and that was all that mattered.

33

BEHIND THE SCENES

"Frank really is a courageous soul," I remarked, as Dana and I darted deeper into the building.

"He is," sighed Dana, and once again I detected that love light in her eyes.

"We have to find Zack," I said, as I studied our surroundings. We were in a red-carpeted corridor, royally decorated with pictures of stars of the stage and screen. People were running in and out of the dozen or so rooms giving out into the corridor. Judging from their appearance—all of them were in diverse states of undress—they were the artists starring in Father Sam's play. And all of them displayed those typical pre-premiere jitters not uncommon with stage artists.

There was a gentleman wearing a tuxedo, a monocle pressed firmly under his left eyebrow, who seemed in excellent spirits, humming a gay tune and smiling a pleasant smile at anyone who cared to look in his direction. He disappeared into a dressing room and I slipped in after him, wondering if perhaps here was where I would find my human. The room was humming with the hustle and bustle of opening night, several extras looking equally spruce in tux and monocle, and all of them talking too loudly and laughing too hard for no reason at all. Conspicuous in his absence, though, was Zack.

I slipped out again. Dana, meanwhile, had checked one of the other dressing rooms and gave me a thumbs down—yes, cats have thumbs. No, they're not opposable ones, but yes, we do have them.

It was at this moment that disaster struck. From a room marked with a golden star—one of the dressing rooms for the stars of the show, I gathered—Barbara Vale suddenly emerged and, seeing Dana, swooped down on her, and scooped her up in her arms. Barbara was a big, motherly woman, with Nana Mouskouri glasses, and a wide, endearing smile that made her cheeks dimple.

"Dana, my pet! What are you doing here?" she squeaked, and before I could intervene, Barbara had disappeared back inside her dressing room, taking Dana along with her. I caught a desperate glance from Dana, and then she was gone. One more soldier was down, and I now faced the enemy alone.

The incident had given me pause, though. If Barbara had her own gold-star dressing room, wouldn't it stand to reason that Zack, too, would be holed up in one? I checked the corridor: only five gold-star rooms left. I sighed. How was I going to get inside? Then I remembered one of the FSA tricks I'd picked up: all I had to do was get inside a human's head and 'nudge' him into action.

I decided to get inside Zack's head and induce him to open his door for me. Closing my eyes and focusing on my human, I willed him to open his door. Opening my eyes, I saw that nothing had happened, apart from a slight headache thrumming behind my left eye. Dang, I still hadn't mastered this particular technique.

Then, remembering Stevie was more proficient at this

than me, I started wondering where my fellow agent and trusted partner could be. Dana and Frank had come running when I'd sent out my distress signal earlier, but Stevie was a no-show, and so was Brutus. That Brutus hadn't heeded my call, I could understand. The cat was, after all, not an FSA agent. But why hadn't Stevie showed up?

I sighed. I only saw one avenue left open for me to pursue, so I pursued it. I ambled over to the first door and gave it a hearty buffet. The door swung open and a red-faced Mayor McCrady popped out. It didn't occur to the chairman of the Brookridge Theatrical Society to look down at little old me, so after scowling down the corridor for a moment, trying to pinpoint the joker who'd played this fool's trick on him and cursing under his breath, he slammed the door closed with a bang that made me jump.

One door down, four more to go. And it was as I'd pounded on door number three, that my luck finally turned. A familiar face popped out of the door and I gave a shriek of elation. I'd found my Zack. Directing his gaze downward, he seemed equally thrilled to see me, for he stooped down and gave me a cuddle, then carried me inside his dressing room. He didn't even seem surprised to see me, but then I could sense that his thoughts were not really with me but with the play.

Attila the Hun could have showed up on his doorstep and he would have bade him entrance, no questions asked, so occupied were his thoughts with the part he was about to play.

Dropping me onto a couch that was conveniently placed against one wall, he started pacing the floor, half-crumpled script pages in his left hand while gesturing wildly with his right.

"Nuts about you!" he vociferated, just a little too loudly.

"And I'll be damned if I'm going to let that little weasel get in the way of our future happiness. Either he goes, or I go!"

With a jolt I recognized the scene I'd seen play out under my elm tree that fateful night, and I knew what would follow. I sat watching, enthralled.

"Either *he* goes, or *I* go," repeated Zack, his arms wide. Typical overacting, I thought.

"Either he *goes*, or I *go*," he said once more, impressing the line upon his memory. He then mumbled something to himself and flipped to another part of the script. "Oh, my darling. My love, love, love." He coughed, closed his eyes and puckered his lips, then made as if to kiss. He grimaced, and I could tell he was thinking about Barbara Vale. He then grabbed a huge knife from his dressing table and started wielding it with uncommon fervor.

"Take that," he cried, as he slashed the air, his face suddenly contorted in rage. "And that, and that, and that!"

Oh, boy. This wasn't good. No, sir. This wasn't good at all.

34

PIPE CLEANING

*J*ust then the stage bell rang, and Zack looked up, as if surprised, the knife temporarily held high above his head. Then he sheathed the monstrosity in a hidden pocket of his coat, abruptly turned a pretty Nile green and, quickly grabbing a wastepaper basket, vomited.

So much for the glory and glamour of the stage artist's life, I thought.

Dabbing at his blue-tinged lips with a cleansing wipe, Zack checked his look in the mirror one last time, then blinked ten times in rapid succession, and vomited again.

Now was this the image of a cold-blooded murderer? I think not. I wracked my brain to figure out what to do next. The best thing would be for Zack not to appear in the play at all. He was an understudy's understudy, so was it so hard to imagine Father Sam had provided for an understudy's understudy's understudy?

Just as I was thinking up ways and means of sabotaging Zack's participation in the play, Father Sam himself suddenly popped his head in the door. He was dressed in some sort of penguin suit, and I remembered he was playing the butler.

"All ready?" Sam said cheerily.

Zack burped. "All ready," he said, though he didn't sound convinced.

"Great," said Sam, beaming. "Just remember, Zack. When Barbara says, 'No, Jack. Don't go,' that's your cue to bring out the knife."

"I'll remember," said Zack, licking his lips and fingering the small sword in his pocket.

"Good man. All right. Break a leg."

"Huh?"

Sam laughed. "Just something we theater folk like to say before going on stage."

"Oh, right," said Zack. "Well, break a leg, too, I guess."

"Thanks," said Sam earnestly, and popped out again.

I was still trying to figure out a way to stop Zack from making a huge mistake, but time was running out, so I simply hopped onto his dressing table, stared into his eyes, and mentally projected the intention he refrain from leaving this room.

For a moment I caught his eye. Then he smiled weakly, patted my head absentmindedly, and abruptly did an about-face and left the room.

I groaned. Total mission failure. And the worst thing was: Zack had closed the door on his way out.

Frantically looking for an escape route, I suddenly noticed an air vent located near the ceiling, its grate dangling from a single screw. A cupboard had been placed under-neath, stocked with boxes of theater paraphernalia. There was a box marked 'wigs', another offering 'beards & mustaches' and a third promising all manner of make-up.

I hopped onto the top of the cupboard, where a nice collection of dust and cobwebs were awaiting me, and from there it was but a single leap to the grate. Hanging on with my claws, I scrabbled up and away into the air duct. Agent Tom had done it again! Now if only this would lead someplace.

I squeezed myself through the duct, which was not built for a cat my size, I might add, and soon found myself facing the tunnel explorer's perennial dilemma: arriving at a crossing, I had the option of going left, right, up, or down. Mh. Difficult decision. I would have preferred to keep going straight, for I had the distinct impression the stage was somewhere ahead of me, but, following my feline intuition, I opted to take a right turn. Unfortunately, my usually unerring intuition had led me astray, for this part of the ventilation system proved a dead end. I now faced what looked like the end of the line for about a yard of dust and one dead rat.

I sneezed and would have scratched my head in bemused puzzlement, if not for the fact that I couldn't move my paws. No wiggle room. With no way of turning round, I had no option but to backpedal. Now, I don't know if any of you have a working knowledge of catdom, but we felines don't come equipped with reverse gears. It was starting to feel really cramped in there, but I suppressed a rising feeling of panic and claustrowhatchamacallit, and willed my limbs to move in the opposite direction.

Oddly enough, they flatly refused. Failure to comply to a direct order, or in other words: mutiny. I broke into a cold sweat at the thought of being stuck there for the rest of my, extremely reduced, life. Oh, and that old wives' tale about the nine lives? Hokum, brother. If this was the end, this was the end. Period.

In frustration I tried wiggling, then jiggling, then wobbling, and finally shimmying. But all to no avail. I was stuck. In desperation, I decided to plunk down on my belly to have a much-needed rest, so I simply retracted my limbs and dropped my bulk onto the 'floor'.

As my belly hit the piping, there was a loud groan, like the death rattle of an expiring piece of equipment, then a clank and a clang, a rending sound, and suddenly the floor gave way and disappeared from under me. The next moment I was hurtling through space, and when I landed, I found myself straddling something soft and hairy. A carpet, or so I thought.

I directed my eyes heavenward and murmured a few choice words of thanks to that great, big Cat in the sky for saving my furry butt. Then I noticed it wasn't a carpet that had broken my fall, but the head of Mayor McCrady. And he didn't seem too well pleased that I'd dug my claws into his skull—what can I say? It's a reflex. The Mayor screamed bloody murder, and lifted both me and his hair—who would have thought the Mayor was wearing a toupee!—into the air, and slung the both of us far and away. Well, at least as far as the stage wings.

I deftly landed on all fours—something that couldn't be said for the toupee—and thanked my lucky stars: the air duct, I now discovered, had been located directly over the prompter's box with the Mayor, who liked to be hands-on when a play was being performed by 'his' Theatrical Society, taking up the role of prompter.

Then, suddenly remembering Zack's big 'murder scene' takes place in the first act, my heart skipped a beat. Was I too late?

35

THE AWFUL TRUTH

Then, to my relief, I saw Zack waiting in the coulisses across from where I'd landed. The big guy was still green around the gills, and his lips kept moving as he repeated his lines over and over again. Next to him I recognized Barbara Vale, apple-cheeked and cheerful as ever, trying to engage Zack in conversation.

She had applied a particularly fluorescent brand of lipstick and now stood puckering her lips in anticipation of the big kissing scene. Zack, catching a glimpse of her, blanched and I could see from the expression on his face his stomach was still doing somersaults.

My relief that I had arrived in time was short-lived as I realized I was running out of time. Short of leaping on stage and taking Zack out with a well-aimed swish of my own retractable knives, thus necessitating the arrival of the stretcher-bearers and ending the performance, I didn't know what to do. Stretcher-bearers being preferable to pallbearers, I had almost decided to go with this gung-ho, yet kamikaze, idea when I noticed another familiar figure high up in the stage rafters.

It was Stevie.

So my fellow agent and FSA partner had made it here after all. The odd thing was, that he wasn't focused on me, but on Zack, staring at my human with a curiously focused intensity.

"Hey, Stevie!" I whispered, but he didn't respond.

I tried to read his mind, but once again couldn't. Then a thought occurred to me: I'd been able to read Zack's mind, hadn't I? Why couldn't I read Stevie's? The only logical answer was that Stevie was blocking me.

The notion frankly startled me. Could it be? Now I remembered that earlier that day I'd tried to read both Stevie's and Dana's mind and had drawn a blank. It all made sense now. Both of them had the capacity to close their minds. With Dana, this seemed obvious. She was a senior agent or officer or whatever her FSA label was. But I'd never have expected Stevie to do the same. Wasn't he a mere trainee, just like me?

Then another thought struck me. Why would Stevie want to block me, unless he was hiding something? He was still staring at Zack with that intense gaze, and then it hit me. Stevie was willing Zack to do something. Nudging him in a certain direction. Had he also figured out Zack was about to use Barbara Vale for fileting practice?

A flood of relief washed over me. Agent Steve to the rescue. My partner had somehow discovered what Zack was about to do, and was trying to stop him. Oh, bless Stevie's heart, I thought. I just hoped he would succeed where I had failed.

Instantly I started making my way up by using the curtains as a climbing pole. Curtains are excellent for this purpose, did you know that? It only took me ten seconds to reach the rail, and from there it was a mere few leaps and bounds to reach my friend and partner. He was sitting between two following spots.

"Ho there, pardner," I said by way of greeting. Stevie had been so focused on Zack—saving the day—that he hadn't noticed my approach. He started violently.

I chuckled freely at his perturbation. "No need to be afraid," I jested. "It's only me. Agent Tom."

"Oh, hi, Tom," he said, though he didn't seem too happy to see me.

I grew serious. These were, after all, serious times. "Any luck changing his mind?" I said, indicating Zack, who now stood on one leg. From our vantage point we had an excellent overview of the action down below on stage.

"What do you mean?" he said nervously.

"Well, trying to convince Zack not to slay the Vale, of course," I said, as if it were the most obvious thing in the world.

He gulped once or twice. "You know about that?"

"Sure," I said, and proceeded to fill him on the state of affairs, omitting no detail, no matter how small.

On stage, Father Sam had appeared in his butler outfit, and was swigging port in what I assumed to be his pantry. He now started singing a song about how he'd lost the girl of his dreams and hoped one day to see her again. I winced and wondered if this was the same singing voice he utilized in church. If so, the piercing whine didn't do him credit.

Stevie, meanwhile, was still gulping like a bullfrog. "So," I concluded, "I made my way here as fast as I could, and have been trying to figure out how to stop Zack since I arrived."

"That's… great," Stevie said, and the comment struck me as rather feeble, as comments go.

"No, it's not," I corrected him. "Haven't you been listening? I tried to dissuade Zack from going down this road, but he didn't respond."

NIC SAINT

"Didn't he?"

Again I was disappointed by his lack of fervor.

"That's why I asked: Have *you* had any luck changing his mind?"

"Me? Um…" His eyes darted to Zack, and I could see them narrowing as he focused his mental powers on my human. Good, at least he was trying hard—very hard—to make Zack… do something that he would normally never, ever do… I frowned. Now, wait a minute, I thought. Something fishy was going on here, something…

And then I got it. The awful truth. Stevie wasn't trying to dissuade Zack from picking up that knife and using it to end Barbara Vale's life. He was willing him to go ahead and do it!

36

THE ATTACK

"Stevie! Stop!" I yelled.

"Huh?" he said, as if waking from a trance. "What's that?"

"You're trying to kill Barbara!"

"I'm doing nothing of the kind," he said, indignant. Then his lips contorted into a wide, toothy grin. "Zack is."

"But why?" was all I could think to say.

He shrugged. "You're smart. You figure it out."

My eyes widened. "You killed Lucy Knicx. And Jamie Burrow!"

He casually studied his paw nails. "Technically Norbert McIlroy did. Though it's safe to say I lent him a paw."

The horror of my partner's betrayal had me reeling, and I nearly plummeted to my death—well, that's probably exaggerating slightly. Cats don't easily plummet to their death, certainly not from a mere 15 feet up. I was just about to repeat my earlier 'But why!' when a brain wave made me see the light. Lucy Knicx. Jamie Burrow. Stevie's comments about how they kept dropping by the house all the time. The eternal fear of any cat that his male human takes in a female human and that the days of wine and roses are about to come to an end...

"You didn't want Lucy or Jamie to take over the run of the house," I said slowly.

Stevie frowned darkly. "Or Barbara, for that matter," he said, confirming I'd hit pay dirt. "Ever since she got the blue belle understudy part, Sam hasn't been able to remove her from the presbytery with a stick."

"But Sam is a priest," I said. "He'll never marry."

"Sam is wavering," Stevie said softly. "All this female attention has had him reconsider his vows. Another couple of months and he would have chucked the church and gone and gotten married to one of these... groupies." He spat out the last word.

"But Barbara is all right," I said. "She's a great human. Just ask Dana."

He shrugged. "Better safe than sorry. Besides, I don't want Dana for a roomie. She'll corner the market on kibble and cuddles and I'll be left fighting for leftovers. No, thank you very much. Now, if you'll excuse me, I've got a Father Sam groupie to eliminate." And he returned to his perch next to the spotlight, and resumed his mental treatment of Zack.

"No, Stevie!" I cried. "Don't do it!"

"Who's gonna stop me?" he scoffed. "You?"

At this moment Zack and Barbara stepped onto the stage. Show time.

"I think he's on to us," said Barbara, taking Zack's lapel in a firm grip.

"Are you sure?" said Zack, after a significant pause.

Barbara gave an unconvincing sob that sounded like a dinosaur removing its foot from a primeval swamp.

"That sucks," said Zack, desperately searching for the prompter. "That means we'll, um, have to, um, whack the sucker."

I was pretty sure this wasn't the way Father Sam had written the scene, but that's show business. No one respects the script.

Barbara hesitated. Her cue had been 'Take him out!', and she was clearly at a loss how to respond to Zack's improv.

"Whack the sucker?" she finally said, though with reluctance. "Are you nuts?"

"Nuts about you!" cried Zack. "And I'll be damned if I'm going to let the little turd come between me and a pretty piece of pecan pie. Um, that's not right," he mumbled.

"No! Jack!" cried Barbara.

"I know, I know," Zack muttered. "He won't come between me and, and... Between me and..." His voice trailed off, as he desperately tried to remember his line. Then he got it, and his face lit up. "Between me and... you! Barbara!"

Barbara closed her eyes. As things were going, it seemed more likely that she'd kill Zack than the other way around.

"No, Jack!" she cried once again, a steely note in her voice. "Don't go!" But the expression on her face belied her words.

Her cry galvanized me into action. I knew what was next, and I could already see Zack's hand steal into his pocket to get a firm grip on the knife handle. So I did the only thing I could think of: I dealt Stevie a hearty smack on the head and, not expecting this, he dropped down to the stage like a ton of bricks. Or rather one brick. Unlike me, Stevie is a lightweight.

On stage, Zack had taken out the knife, and held it out behind Barbara's back, in full view of the audience, which collectively gasped in shocked surprise. When one attends the performance of a murder mystery play, one obviously expects a murder, and Zack was about to give the public its money's worth of blood and gore.

Stevie landed deftly on all fours, but his landing platform, unlike mine, wasn't Mayor McCrady's soft hairpiece, but

Barbara Vale's bare back. Digging in his claws to prevent his further descent, Stevie finally got his wish and drew Vale blood. The bone-chilling scream that next rent the air, had the audience once again rocket back in their chairs, cries of anguish and horror on their lips, for Barbara didn't stint on volume.

"You idiot!" she screamed, and, swinging her purse like a hammer, she let it come down hard on Zack's head, for she had automatically jumped to the conclusion Zack must have nicked her with that big, shiny knife of his.

Stevie, rightly deducing he wasn't wanted on the scene at this particular moment, quickly made good his escape.

"Ouch!" Zack yelled, as Barbara's purse impacted on his head. He dropped the knife.

Now, when a knife drops to the floor, it usually makes a clanking sound. This particular knife, though, hit the floor with its pointy end, and simply bounced back up, before landing on its hilt, bouncing a few more times and then coming to rest, tired of all these theatrical shenanigans.

I had seen the knife bounce and I had seen it plunk down, and I sat back on my high perch above the stage with a sinking feeling in the pit of my stomach, grabbing onto one of the spotlights to keep me from keeling over and plunging into the abyss.

For I'd just realized that this was not the kind of knife that slays ten in a murdering frenzy. This was a stage knife, and what was more, made of rubber. No way could Zack have done any harm to Barbara, even if he'd wanted to. At most he could have smudged her dress.

"What—what—what—" I stammered, as I stared before me with unseeing eyes. "W-w-what the *heck* is going on?"

AGENT TOM

*I*t was at this moment that I became aware I wasn't alone up there. The air to my left suddenly seemed to shimmer, like it does on a hot summer's day, and even before a bright flash popped and she appeared out of nowhere, I knew I was in the presence of Dana. She had a vague smile on her lips.

"Hello, Tom," she said.

Then the same thing happened again, but this time to my right. A loud pop, and there he sat, cool as dammit and grinning gaily: Stevie. He actually looked more like the old Stevie I'd come to know and, well, yes, almost love.

I shook my head, dazed and confused. What was going on here?

On stage, meanwhile, the murder mystery had turned into a farce, with Barbara chasing Zack around the set, using all manner of props to hurl at him. The audience members were now rolling in the aisles, laughing their collective heads off. I don't know how Father Sam would feel about all this, and frankly, I didn't care. What I wanted to know was…

"What's going on? That's what you wanted to ask, right?" said Dana softly.

I merely nodded, still feeling rather dazed. "Let me get this straight," I began, but that's as far as I got. Nothing was straight.

"You're on candid camera," said Stevie, who was crouching low and holding onto the steel girder with a death grip. Together with the old Stevie, his fear of heights had also made a comeback. Probably being plunked on the back of the head by yours truly hadn't helped.

"Am I?" I said, searching around for the cameras.

"Shut up, Stevie," said Dana. "No, you're not," she said to me.

I looked down, where Zack and Barbara had left the stage, and a wise stage manager had drawn the curtains. Barbara, who was supposed to be dead by the end of act 1, was still very much alive. I could hear her screaming all the way from her dressing room. I briefly wondered how the play would start act 2 without a murder to investigate or a dead body to examine.

"Huh?" I said, for I perceived that Dana was addressing me.

"I said, this must all be very confusing for you."

I said she was right.

"It was all a test," said Stevie blithely. He clapped me on the back. "We all go through it."

"Huh?" I repeated.

Dana gave Stevie a look of disapproval. "Shut up, Stevie."

"Oh, all right," said Stevie, rolling his eyes. "Just saying."

"Huh?" I said a third time.

"Stevie's right," said Dana. "Everything you've experienced these last couple of days has been one big recruitment exercise. And I'm glad to say that you've passed the test with flying colors, Tom."

I didn't even have the oomph to say 'Huh' again, so I merely goggled.

"The FSA stages these exercises for every recruit. Just a way to make sure we're not inducting anyone into our ranks who doesn't justify the expenditure."

I cleared my throat with some difficulty. "Expenditure?" I said.

"Sure," said Dana. "Now that you're cleared for admission, we're starting up your training."

"And I'm going with," said Stevie. "Finally."

"Stevie was inducted a little over a month ago," said Dana. "But we've been waiting for a fifth recruit before organizing training camp. You're number five."

"There's four more like—" I glanced over at Stevie. "—him?"

"Don't be so shocked," said Stevie, grinning. "You sound as if you don't like me."

"Oh, I like you all right," I said. "I just don't know if I can trust you."

He slung an arm around my shoulders. "Oh, bro, don't be that way. I was just playing along with Dana's little scheme."

"Were you now?" I said frostily. I still hadn't forgiven him for lying to me. "Partners should have no secrets from one another," I reminded him. "They should tell each other everything."

He looked at me in mock reproof. "But I *do* tell you everything. Just not the part about this all being one big training op."

"Just that part, huh? You're quite the actor, you know that? Stringing me along like that, while all the time you knew exactly what was going on. No fair."

He beamed. "You think so? About the actor part? That was part of my training."

I made a face, and he held up his paws, palms up.

"Stevie's right," said Dana. "Part of being a secret agent is to be able to convincingly construct an entirely fictitious persona and present it to the world. I think Stevie did a great job."

"You mean I will have to do… this… as well?" I said, incredulously.

Dana smiled. "You've already begun."

"Me? No way," I said.

"Sure you have. Don't you remember your little tête-à-tête with Brutus?"

"Brutus is going to be an FSA recruit?" I said, aghast.

"You'll have a ball," said Stevie. "That cat is so gullible, you wouldn't believe it. He actually thought Dollo Rosso was a Southridge gangster. Can you beat it?"

He laughed heartily. I didn't join him. The prospect of having to team up with Brutus didn't appeal to me, and I said as much to Dana.

She shrugged. "That's part of the job description, Tom. If you want to be a feline spy, you can't always choose the people you deal with. Some of them will become great friends, like Stevie here—"

I gave Stevie a look that indicated his friendship status was temporarily on hold.

"—while others will be really nasty specimen."

"James Bond wasn't buddy-buddy with Goldfinger, was he?" said Stevie, stung that I hadn't acknowledged our great friendship. "Or those guys from SPECTRE? Well, then?"

I decided to change the subject. "What happened to Lucy Knicx? And Jamie Burrow?"

Dana smiled. "Lucy's in bed with a cold. Lying on the park ground that night didn't do her much good."

"So the 'ghost' we heard…"

"Was in fact Frank," said Dana. "He's getting better at this stuff. As far as Jamie is concerned, she has a new boyfriend and decided spending time with him was more important than playing the part of Zoe Huckleberry."

"But what about the body I saw in the park yesterday?"

"That wasn't a body," said Dana, "but a lifelike doll. Every year the Brookridge police department, in cooperation with the Red Cross, teaches a refresher course in CPR for drowning victims and other first aid techniques. I made sure the exercise was over by the time we got there. All the members of the public had gone home and the people you saw were about to pack up and leave with the 'body.'"

"So that's why they didn't seem interested in the victim," I said, understanding dawning. "But what about Rick Mascarpone and Norbert McIlroy? Weren't they supposed to be here tonight?"

"Rick Mascarpone doesn't exist," said Dana.

"I came up with that name," said Stevie proudly.

"And Norbert McIlroy decided to stay home with Lucy and the kids. He's Lucy Knicx's husband, by the way. That's why they were in the park that night. They'd gone to see a movie together—Jamie Burrow was babysitting if I'm not mistaken—and decided to take a stroll through the park and practice their lines."

"But you couldn't have possibly known all that," I said.

Dana shrugged. "Part of the job is perfect planning, and the other part is knowing how to improvise. When I saw Lucy and Norbert that night, I figured it was a good way to start you on your process. The rest worked itself out as we went along."

The three of us sat in silence for a spell. On stage the curtains had opened once again, and Zack and Barbara were repeating the murder scene. Good idea. Without a murder, they could just as well throw out the whole play and call it a night.

I tried to read Dana and Stevie's minds as we sat watching

Zack stumble through his lines, but they wouldn't let me. Blocked. I really wanted to know how to do that.

"You'll learn," said Dana.

Cripes. I wish she would stop doing that.

"All right," said Dana. "I won't do it again."

This raised yet more questions. For instance, how could I be certain she wouldn't? It was not as if I had a way of knowing who was taking a peek inside my brain.

"You'll know," Stevie said.

Aargh!

Stevie merely giggled.

❧

So there. That's my life. The life of a junior feline spy. Having to team up with bullies. Having my mind read by Ragamuffins, Siamese and—now that I come to think of it—probably Poodles as well. Being snarled at by extremely disagreeable Peterbalds. Seeing dead bodies everywhere that aren't dead bodies after all. And saving humans that don't need saving.

If you ask me what I learned from all this? Well, that even though those humans didn't need saving, lending a helping hand made *me* feel good. Looking back at the Brookridge Park horror, I guess I went from being an egotist and a little bit of a fathead—

"Nothing little about it. You were a major fathead," remarked Stevie.

Will you please stay away from my brain, Stevie?

"Oh, all right."

Now where was I? Ah, yes. I went from being a minor fathead to—

"Being a major fathead," said Stevie, with a guffaw.

"Stevie!" said Dana.

"But he's asking for it!" protested Stevie.

"If you can't respect your partner's private space, consider yourself suspended from active duty. Is that what you want? No? Then please behave."

"Some partner," grumbled Stevie. "Can't even take an innocent little joke."

So. Recapitulating here for a moment. I went from being a selfish fathead—that all right with you, Stevie?—to realizing how much humans mean to me, and wanting, more than anything, to save them from harm. In other words, I went from being an egotist to being an altruist. Of sorts. That about covers it, Dana?

"It does," said Dana, well pleased. "You can consider yourself recruited, Agent Tom.

"Finally," sighed Stevie.

"Finally," I agreed.

THE END

EXCERPT FROM PURRFECT MURDER (THE MYSTERIES OF MAX 1)

Chapter One

I lifted one eyelid and grunted approvingly at the sun bathing the room in its golden hue. It was eight o'clock in the morning, so high time for an extended nap, but first I needed to see my human off to work. As usual, Odelia had a hard time throwing off the blanket of sleep and facing the world. She was still in bed, even though her alarm clock had gone off, and I'd alerted her to the fact that a new day was dawning by meowing plaintively and as loud as I possibly could, pawing the wardrobe door in the process. She'd thrown a throw pillow at me, so I knew she'd gotten the message.

It wouldn't be long now. Odelia might hate getting up in the morning, but eventually she inevitably does, so I stretched and rolled over onto my back.

I have to admit I really lucked out when I was selected by Odelia to become her pet eight years ago, when she picked me out of the litter and decided I was a keeper. Odelia is not only one of the nicest and most decent humans a cat could ever hope to get, but she's also very generous when it comes to distributing the kibble and other goodies. She keeps my bowl filled to the rim, and frequently adds a tasty wet food surprise to the mix.

My name is Max, by the way, and as you might have guessed I'm a feline. A male feline. Some of my friends call me fat, but that is simply a vicious lie. I'm big-boned. All the tabbies in my family are. It's genetics. And, just like my brothers and sisters, I'm blorange. A blend of orange and blond.

Today was going to be a special day. I could feel it in my bones. Yes, my big bones. But it wasn't merely my intuition. Harriet, the white Persian belonging to Odelia's parents who live next door, told me last night that a new cop had moved to Hampton Cove. And if she hadn't told me I would have found out for myself, for there was a new cat on the block. A nasty brute aptly called Brutus. Black as coal, built like Tom Brady, and with evil green eyes, Brutus barged into our midnight meeting in Hampton Cove Park last night, announcing he was now in charge of all the public spaces in Hampton Cove, on account of the fact that his owner was a cop. Delusions of grandeur was what I called it, and in response Brutus demonstrated the sharpness of his claws by stripping a nice piece of bark from my favorite tree.

Not a cat you want to rumble with, in other words. And if his owner was made of the same cloth, the town of Hampton Cove was in for a rough ride.

"Hey, Max," Odelia's voice rang out as she descended the stairs.

"Over here," I said, giving her a wave from my position on the couch.

She plunked herself down next to me and gave my belly a

tickle. She was still dressed in pink PJs, rubbing the sleep from her eyes with one hand while she rubbed my belly with the other. In response, I purred contentedly.

Odelia is slim and trim, with shoulder-length blond hair and big eyes the color of seaweed that always sparkle with the light of intelligence. She grimaced when a ray of sunshine hit her face. "Wow, too much too soon."

"Not really," I said. "Sun's been up since before seven, sleepyhead."

"You don't have to rub it in," she said, getting up with a groan. "I was up late last night working on a piece about that sinkhole on Hayes Road."

She shuffled into the kitchen and started up the coffeemaker while I tripped after her, then hopped onto one of the kitchen counter stools so we could continue our conversation. Oh, didn't I mention it? Odelia belongs to that rare kind of human who can actually converse with cats. Not that she's Doctor Dolittle or something, but she comes from a long line of women with a strong affinity with the feline species. As far as I understand it, her foremothers were witches, at a time when being a witch was a surefire way of getting burned at the stake. And even though that witchy streak has diminished over the generations, the women in her family can talk to cats, and do so to their heart's content. Odelia even claims her ancestors used to turn themselves into cats and back. No idea if that's true but it's pretty cool.

I glanced at my bowl, and saw it was still half full, which was better than half empty, so I returned my attention to Odelia, who was pouring cornflakes into her own bowl. Yikes. How she can eat that stuff, I don't know.

"Did you hear the latest?" I asked, draping my tail around my buttocks.

"No, what's that?"

"There's a new cop in town."

This seemed to interest her, for she looked up from her cereal. "Oh?"

"Yeah, some hotshot that calls himself Chase Kingsley. Used to work for the NYPD."

"The NYPD? So what's he doing in Hampton Cove?"

I shrugged. Yes, cats can shrug, though it's hard to notice with all the hair. "Beats me. All I know is that people are saying he might succeed Chief Alec."

Odelia frowned. "That's impossible. Uncle Alec is only…" She frowned some more. "Actually I have no idea how old he is."

"He's older than your mother," I supplied.

"Yeah, but not old enough to retire, surely."

"I don't know. Maybe he wants to take early retirement."

"I'll have to ask him," she said, making a mental note of this.

Odelia works for the *Hampton Cove Gazette* as a reporter, and I give her the odd scoop now and then. Since us cats are pretty much all over the place, I've been able to provide her with a steady stream of breaking news over the years, ranging from that rat infestation at Dough Knot Bakery, to the milk spill at the dairy farm. Cats were all over that one, as you can imagine.

This has given Odelia's career quite a boost, and given her the reputation of a hard-nosed reporter. Her editor often asks her where she gets her information, but she's been diligently protecting her sources—*moi*. If word ever got out that her sources all have whiskers, a furry tail and a propensity for licking their own genitalia, she'd probably be front-page news herself.

"I should probably do an interview with this Chase Kingsley."

She took a tentative sip from her coffee and perked up. It's something I've never understood about humans. How they can drink that horrible brew. I've jumped up on this kitchen counter once or twice to have a lick at the stuff, and I can't get over the terrible taste. I'll take a piece of chicken liver every time.

"You should. I hear he's one of those hunkishly handsome guys."

She looked up at this. "Hunkishly handsome?"

"And single, if the word on the street is to be believed. At least that's what Harriet told me." I shook my head disgustedly. "Probably one of those playboy types who goes around hitting on every woman in sight."

"I'll bet he's not," said Odelia, taking the next seat.

"Oh, yes, he is. If Harriet is mooning over Chase Kingsley you can rest assured he's the playboy type. She's always falling for that kind of guy."

"She can't fall for that kind of guy," said Odelia, making a funny face. "Harriet is a cat, Max. Cats don't fall for humans. It's simply not possible."

"Oh, yes, they do. Cats fall for humans all the time, only not for the same reason humans fall for other humans. When we fall for one of you it's because you provide us with a great home, great food and great cuddles."

"And why does Harriet think this Chase Kingsley provides all of that?"

"Because he's got a cat of his own. A nasty brute called Brutus. I met him last night and he's a real piece of work. And if his owner is anything like him, we've got another thing coming in this town. Do you know what he told me?"

She took a swig from her coffee. "What?"

I lowered my voice. "He only eats meat. No kibble. Can you believe it?"

She laughed. "Sounds to me like you're jealous, Max."

"Hey, I'm the least jealous cat in this town."

"Why does eating meat make Brutus a bad cat?"

"Because... who gives their cat only raw meat? It's simply not done!"

She nodded. "Who's got the money, right?"

"Exactly. You certainly don't." If this came across as a barb, I didn't mean it. I totally get how Odelia can't afford to feed me filet mignon every day. Not on a reporter's salary.

But if I expected her to be offended, I was mistaken. Instead, a keen look had appeared in her eyes. "Do you think this Chase Kingsley is rich?"

"I doubt it. A cop? Rich? Highly unlikely."

"Maybe he comes from money?"

I shook my head. "I don't think so, honey. If he did, either Brutus or Harriet would have told me. The guy's a genuine blabbermouth, and so is Harriet, as you well know."

"Know what?" asked a voice from the door.

Chapter Two

Oh, crap. That's the problem with cats. They tread so softly you never hear them coming until they're already upon you.

"Hey, Harriet," I said when the white Persian strode into the kitchen. As usual, she was looking haughty, her nose in the air. I swear she thinks she's the Queen of Sheba or something. Or the Queen of Hampton Cove, at least.

"We were just saying how well-informed you always are," said Odelia.

Nice save. "Yeah, how you always seem to know everything about everybody," I added sweetly.

She smiled at this. You might be surprised that cats can smile, but they can. Again, it's the hair. It obscures many of our facial tics. "It's true," she said complacently. "I do know everything about everybody all of the time."

"Max was just telling me about this new cop in town," said Odelia.

"Chase Kingsley," she said, nodding. "He's a dreamboat."

"Oh, God," I groaned. "Here we go again."

"No, he is," she insisted. "He's just about the most handsome man I've ever laid eyes on, and I've laid eyes on my fair share of men over the years."

Listening to Harriet, you would almost think she's a human herself, which is a phenomenon quite common amongst cats. They spend so much time with humans they get confused. It's called cross-species confusion. It's a thing. It really is. At least I think it is. "If he's as handsome as Brutus, I can tell you you're blind, Harriet," I said now. "That guy isn't handsome. He's scary."

"There's nothing scary about Brutus," she said huffily. "He's one fine cat."

"He's a bully, that's what he is, and I don't like him one bit. Barging in here as if he owns the place." Then suddenly it dawned on me what Harriet had said. I narrowed my eyes at her. "How would you know what Chase Kingsley looks like? Did you see him?"

"I sure did." Her face took on a beatific quality. "He looks lovely when he sleeps. Like an incredibly buff angel."

Odelia barked an incredulous laugh. "You watched him sleep?"

"Of course. I walked Brutus home last night and he invited me in. Who was I to say no? Especially when it gave me the chance to get a glimpse of the new cop in town. And I have to say Chase Kingsley is everything Brutus said he was and more." She emitted a giggle. "He sleeps in his boxers. No PJs."

If I could have, I would have covered my ears with my paws. "Please, Harriet. Don't make me puke."

"He sleeps in his boxers?" asked Odelia.

Harriet gave her tail a studious lick. "Boxers... and nothing more. Très cute."

I held up my paw. "Enough already. Brutus is a bully and I'm pretty sure so is his master. Or have you forgotten that pets and their owners often share distinctive traits?"

"Oh, please. Odelia's blond and you're orange."

"Blorange. I'm blorange, which is almost the same thing as blond."

"I'm sure that's not even a real color."

"It is a color," I assured her. "It's strawberry blond, with gold rose hues."

"You're such a freak," Harriet sighed, shaking her snowy white fur.

"Hey, don't use the word freak in my house," warned Odelia. "That's not nice. Now tell me more about this new cop. Where does he live?"

"He's staying at Chief Alec's for the moment. Until he can find his own place."

Odelia's eyes were positively glittering with interest. So I gave her a warning scowl. "Don't listen to Harriet. The guy is a bully. Waltzing into town as if he owns the place. Leaving his repulsive pee all over the place."

Odelia frowned. "Leaving his pee? You mean Chase Kingsley is a public urinator? That's not right for a cop. Or anyone else for that matter."

"Not Kingsley, Brutus. Though I wouldn't put it past Kingsley either."

"How would you know? You haven't even met the guy," Harriet challenged.

"I just know these things. I'm a great judge of character."

"You're simply jealous because both Brutus and Chase are alpha males and you're not."

"They're bullies," I pointed out. "There's a distinction."

She turned to Odelia. "You should snap him up now, Odelia, if you want to have a shot at him. He's bound to become very popular very soon."

This appeared to be one bridge too far for Odelia, though. "I have no intention whatsoever to snap anyone up," she said, her smile vanishing. "The only reason I'm asking is because I'll need to write a piece about the guy."

"I'm sure Chief Alec will drop by the newspaper today to introduce him," Harriet said, then lowered her gaze. "So you better make sure you're dressed to the nines, honey. Remember what they say about first impressions."

"Odelia doesn't have to dress up to make a great first impression," I said. "And what's more, I don't see why she has to make a great first impression in the first place. It's not as if she's even remotely interested in the man, is she?" I gave Odelia a pointed look, but she chose to ignore me. Never a good sign.

"I can always make an extra effort," she said instead, dragging her fingers through her long blond mane and shaking it out until it fanned out across her shoulders. Uh-oh.

"Why would you want to dress up for that idiot?" I asked, alarmed.

She laughed. "You're overreacting, Max. I just want to make sure I look presentable for our first meeting. I'll probably spend a considerable amount of time with the man, working closely together as I have with Uncle Alec."

That was true enough. As a reporter, she often sat together with the chief to thresh out the details of some case he was working on.

She now rose from the chair and drained the final dregs from her cup, then transferred it to the sink and gave it a good rinse. "Think I'll go and get ready, you guys." She winked at Harriet. "Don't want to be late for work."

Harriet purred approvingly. The moment Odelia had disappeared upstairs, Harriet gave me a supercilious look. "See? She likes him already. That's women's intuition for you."

"Oh, boy," I muttered. I had a bad feeling about this. Odelia hooking up with this cop? No way. Imagine they hit it off. Next thing they'd be moving in together, which meant I'd have to share my space with Brutus. Not only my space, but my food, too. And my extra special place at the foot of the bed!

"Trouble in paradise?" asked Harriet sweetly. Too sweetly for my taste.

"I can't move in with that Nazi furball, Harriet," I said, shaking my head nervously. "I can't live with the monster bully spawn from hell!"

"I told you, he's not a bully, Max. Brutus is simply a stickler for discipline. Just like his human, I would imagine. They're both cops, Max, not bullies."

But I wasn't fooled. Last night Brutus had sprayed all over my favorite tree, just to taunt me. When I complained, he pointed out that Hampton Cove Park and its trees were part of the public domain, and as such off limits to cats that weren't law enforcement like him. If I wanted to mark a tree as my own, I would have to do it in my own backyard, not the park. It was an awfully narrow interpretation of the Hampton Cove penal code, I felt, if cat spraying was even in the code, as Brutus seemed to suggest.

"He practically chased us out of the park last night!" I cried.

"He did nothing of the kind. He simply pointed out that we're not supposed to view the park as part of our personal territory."

"He said I should stick to my backyard if I want to mark my territory!"

"Well, isn't your backyard big enough for you? And if you're so desperate for space you can pee in my yard, too, Max. All right? *Mi jardin es su jardin.*"

"I don't even know what that means," I grumbled. Or actually I did. It meant that from now on, this town wasn't ours anymore. Brutus had taken over.

"Hey, you guys," a voice spoke from the living room. "Where are you?"

I rolled my eyes again, and Harriet had to suppress a giggle.

"Over here, Dooley!" I called out, then heaved an exasperated groan.

The Ragamuffin came waddling up. "Oh, hey," he said, his usual stupid grin plastered all over his stupid face.

Dooley is Odelia's grandmother's cat, and he's not exactly the sharpest tool in the shed. In fact he's probably the dumbest cat for miles around, which hasn't stopped him from securing himself a place in the Poole clan's hearts and minds. He's a big, beige, fluffy hairball, and seems to have gotten it into his head that I'm his best friend and wingman. Probably because he lives next door, and is in here all the time. In that sense Harriet, Dooley and I are one big, happy family. Or at least that's how Dooley sees it.

"What were you talking about?" he asked now.

"The new cat in town," I said before I could stop myself.

Dooley's eyes widened. "There's a new cat in town?"

"Brutus," Harriet said. "Remember from last night? We met at the park?"

"He told you not to rub yourself against your favorite tree," I added.

"Oh, that Brutus," he said, his face clearing. "What about him?"

"Harriet seems to think he's something special," I said. "While I think he's the second coming of Satan, Lucifer and the Prince of Darkness combined."

Dooley shivered. "I thought he was way intense."

I gestured at Dooley. "Thank you, Dooley. Brutus *is* intense."

Harriet didn't agree, of course. "Perhaps it's because he has taken on so much responsibility. That kind of pressure can weigh on a cat."

"What responsibility!" I cried. "He's just a stupid cat!"

"He does have great fur, though," said Dooley.

I turned to him. "What?!"

"That's raw meat for you," said Harriet, a little enviously.

"He gets raw meat?" asked Dooley, surprised.

"Only raw meat," I agreed grudgingly.

"No wonder he's so incredibly buff and fit!" said Dooley.

"He is buff and fit, isn't he?" gushed Harriet. "He's simply dreamy."

"He's a musclebound moron," I grumbled. "That's what he is."

"Who is a musclebound moron?" asked Odelia, stepping into the kitchen. She'd showered and dressed and looked cute as a button in a flowery summer dress that revealed quite a bit of cleavage and a lot of leg. My jaw dropped. If this was the way she was going to meet Chase Kingsley I might as well welcome Brutus into our home now. The guy would fall for her like a ton of bricks. I just knew he would. No one could resist my human when she was all fresh-faced and cute as a button like this.

"Brutus," I said, in a last-ditch effort to stop this terrible ordeal from taking place. "Like his master, he's a musclebound idiot addicted to meat."

"You can't be addicted to meat," Dooley laughed. "It's an

essential component of a well-balanced diet. And what's essential can't be addictive."

"Yeah, yeah," I grunted. "Thank you, Dr. Phil."

Dooley blinked confusedly. "Who's Dr. Phil?"

"You guys better behave," said Odelia as she snatched her clutch from the counter and strode to the sliding door that led into the backyard. She closed it. "Oh, and could you find out whatever you can about Chase Kingsley?"

Now it was my turn to blink confusedly. "Anything?"

"Sure. The more I know about him, the better... for my article," she concluded lamely.

I saw an opportunity here. An opportunity to dig up some dirt on this new supercop, so I nodded. "Sure. I'll do my best."

"Great. See you later, guys."

"See you, hon," said Harriet.

"See you, Odelia," said Dooley.

I didn't say anything. I was thinking hard how to stop my human from hooking up with Brutus's human and making my worst nightmare come true.

We watched Odelia walk out the front door, then return five seconds later to grab her sunglasses from the hallway credenza, then return again to grab her smartphone, give us a goofy grin, a cheery wave, and pull the door shut.

"Oh, don't look so glum," said Harriet.

"You would look glum if you were about to be kicked out of your home."

"Brutus won't kick you out of your home."

"He will, too. First he kicked me out of the park, now he'll kick me out of my house. The cat's a genuine natural born bully."

"He's not. He's simply... a natural born leader."

"And what does that make me? A natural born loser?"

Harriet merely grinned.

"Oh, I can see what's going on here," I said. "Odelia is hooking up with hot new cop, and you're hooking up with hot new cat. Is that it?"

She shrugged and sashayed in the direction of the pet door. "Time for my beauty nap, boys. See you later." And with a swish of her tail, she gracefully disappeared through the door and was gone, leaving me alone with Dooley.

"So who's this Dr. Phil?" Dooley asked after a pregnant pause.

"Oh... just go away, Dooley."

Chapter Three

I resisted the temptation to take a long nap on my favorite blanket, the one Odelia had put on the couch to protect it from my habit of digging my nails into any soft tissue I encountered. I needed to check out this cop character first. If this guy decided to put the moves on my human and foist Brutus on me, I needed to stop him dead in his tracks before that happened.

So I bade goodbye to Dooley and waddled out the pet door and into the backyard. After sniffing at a couple of trees, just to make sure no one had dared trespass on my domain, I set out along the road, slowly making my way into town. It didn't take me long to reach the police station, which was just around the corner. I knew it as the place where cops liked to gather to snack on glazed donuts and coffee before starting their job of catching bad humans.

Not that there are a lot of bad humans in Hampton Cove. In fact it's probably the most peaceful town on the North Shore. Apart from your occasional rowdy tourist collapsing on the beach or wrapping his car around a tree, it's a pretty peaceful little town, and we like to keep it that way.

I hurried across the road, narrowly being missed by a

speeding car, past the doctor's office where Odelia's dad Tex works, and the library, where her mom works as a librarian, and finally reached town square, with the giant clock the mayor had installed a couple of years ago and which has proved such a hit with locals and tourists alike, and then I was homing in on the police station. A squat one-story building, it sported the letters 'Hampton Cove Police Department' above the entrance. Behind those double doors, Dolores sat, presiding over the vestibule and always ready to take note of any complaint the citizenry might have. Since technically I wasn't part of the citizenry, and couldn't very well waltz in through the front door, I walked around back instead, and headed straight for the window of Chief Alec's office, where I'd picked up many a private conversation over the years.

I hopped up onto the windowsill and once again praised Chief Alec's good sense always to leave the window open a crack. Someone must have told him once that fresh air was good for him, and I could only agree wholeheartedly.

One peek inside the office of the good chief told me that I'd hit the jackpot. He was in there with a hunkish male I'd never seen before. His long limbs stretched out languidly, his athletic body casually draped across the chair, he was listening to Chief Alec intently. He was definitely a handsome guy. He had one of those square jaws and chiseled faces that were all the rage with the ancient Greeks. A lock of dark brown hair dangled down his brow, his hair a little too long for a cop, which gave him a rebellious look.

His white cotton shirt was stretched taut over bulging chest muscles, and his arms were all biceps and triceps and his belly was perfectly flat, unlike the beer belly Chief Alec had going for himself. If I'd had to venture a guess, I'd have pegged the guy in his early thirties, and never had the words 'ruggedly handsome' been a better description for any human male. Odelia was definitely in trouble, if my limited experience was anything to go on.

I hunkered down and pricked up my ears, hoping to find confirmation that this guy was, indeed, Chase Kingsley, and not simply a tourist filing a complaint about a stolen wallet, or a traveling salesman badgering the chief.

"So what do we know so far?" the guy was saying.

"I just called the ME's office," said Chief Alec, "and they told me they're expecting the results from the autopsy some-time this morning."

The chief, a mainstay in this town for over thirty years, was the embodiment of law and order. He was also a very large man, easily twice as big as the man seated across from him. Everyone knew him as a kind-hearted, fair-minded police officer, never one to throw his weight around. He liked to settle disputes with a smile and a kindly word, ever the courteous diplomat.

And then it dawned on me. Autopsy? Had someone died? I turned my antennae-like ears toward the window, my eyes narrowed in concentration.

"Good thing Adele Pun found the body. The poor guy might never have been found otherwise," said the one I assumed was Chase Kingsley.

"You're right about that, Chase," grunted the chief.

Bingo! I stared at Brutus's owner, and couldn't resist uttering a growl.

"That body was never meant to be found, and if the Pun woman hadn't gone snooping around, the killer would have pulled off the perfect crime."

I blinked. Killer? Crime? Oh. My. God. They were talking murder!

"So how did Adele Pun discover the body?" asked Chase.

The chief barked a curt, humorless laugh. "Well, that's a

writer for you, Chase. They will go sticking their noses where they don't belong."

At this, the chief directed a long, lingering look at me, and I froze. Not that I minded too much. Chief Alec was Odelia's uncle on her mother's side, after all, and I was pretty sure he was aware of his sister and niece's secret.

He looked away again, and continued his story. "She says she was taking a dump a couple of days ago and suddenly started wondering where the product of her bowel movements went. Curious, she went and got herself a flashlight, to examine the bottom of the well, and shone it down into the abyss where generations of Hampton Covians have done their thing."

"You should have been a poet, Chief," remarked Chase dryly.

"Thank you. Imagine her surprise when she discovered a laptop sticking out of the tranquil surface of the brown pool below. Being a writer, holed up at a writer's lodge, she naturally wondered what that laptop was doing there."

Chase made a disgusted face. "Don't tell me. She retrieved the laptop?"

The chief grinned. "She most certainly did. Though I have no idea how she did it. I imagine she used a shovel or a rake or something. Then she put the garden hose on it and dumped it into a bucket of salt for three days."

"And what? It booted up?"

"It sure did. Just goes to show those cheap Korean laptops are a lot sturdier than you'd give them credit for. Reminds me never to spend two thousand bucks on a computer ever again."

"And that's how she discovered it was Paulo Frey's laptop."

"Yes, sir. None other than the elusive Mr. Frey."

"The missing writer."

"The missing writer," the chief agreed.

I almost fell off the sill at this point. Paulo Frey was a famous novelist who'd gone missing some time last year. He'd been in the habit of renting the Writer's Lodge once a year, a fixed-up old cabin in the woods on the edge of Hampton Cove. It was popular with writers, as there were no distractions out there, and they could work on their master-pieces undisturbed. There was even an old-fashioned outhouse, which for some reason seemed to appeal to the writing classes. Many a writer confessed they got their best ideas while seated on the john and allowing nature to run its course. Weird but true.

Paulo Frey had been one of those writers who felt they could only write a decent novel while ensconced at the Writer's Lodge, pecking away at his laptop. Until he'd myste-riously vanished. The owner of the lodge—Hetta Fried—a patron of the arts—had assumed he'd simply skipped town, but when he hadn't shown up in New York, his relatives had sounded the alarm.

The cabin had been thoroughly searched, but Paulo hadn't left a trace, so no foul play was assumed. It wasn't as if he hadn't pulled a stunt like this before. Once he'd upped and left and had shown up six months later in Zimbabwe, living quietly in a hut in the jungle, trying to cure a severe case of writer's block. He was one of those eccentric writers, the ones they make movies about with Johnny Depp in the lead.

"So Adele notified the police," said Chase.

"She notified me," the chief acknowledged. "At which point we decided to take a closer look at that outhouse."

Chase shook his head. "That must be the last outhouse on Long Island."

"It may very well be," the chief agreed. "It's garnered a lot of praise from writers. Supposed to give them ideas. Kinda like a wishing well. You drop in a nickel and you get to make a wish. Only here you drop in something else."

"So when did you get the idea to dredge the well?"

"Well, at first we figured Frey had simply hurled his laptop into the pit in a fit of rage or something. Which would fit with the writer's block theory." The chief shifted his bulk, making his chair creak dangerously. "But after poking around in there for a bit, something else came bobbing up." He fixed Chase with a knowing glance. "An arm."

"Yikes."

"Yeah. So we called in a cesspool pumping service and found—"

"Paulo Frey."

"Along with all of his stuff, stuffed into three Louis Vuitton suitcases. All packed and ready to go... nowhere. Looks like whoever killed him wanted to make it look like he skipped town, while he was stuffed down there all along."

"I wouldn't like to be the ME on this one," said Chase, wrinkling his nose.

"You said it," said the chief, shaking his head. "This is one messy business."

"When will you know more?"

The chief checked the clock over the door. It was one of those clocks that wouldn't have looked out of place in a classroom. "Shouldn't be long now. We don't get a lot of homicides here, so they've given this their highest priority. I'm expecting a call before lunch." He patted the desk. "So what about it, Chase? Are you ready to work your first Hampton Cove homicide case?"

Chase grinned. "Throwing me in at the deep end, huh, Chief?"

"Best way to learn, buddy."

"What better way indeed?"

At this point in the conversation, I hopped down from the

windowsill and landed gracefully on all fours on the flagged floor. I'd heard enough. A genuine homicide! In Hampton Cove! This was a scoop that needed to be on the front page of the next edition of the *Hampton Cove Gazette*. Pronto! And who better to break the story to our loyal readership than star reporter Odelia Poole herself? This would cement her reputation as the town's best-informed reporter. Wait till I told her about this. She'd be over the moon.

And wait was exactly what I had to do, for as I made my way to the street, I found my passage blocked by a stocky, burly black cat with evil green eyes. Brutus!

"Snooping around, are we, Max?" he asked in a sneering manner. At that moment he suddenly reminded me of Draco Malfoy, Harry Potter's nemesis.

Oh, God. This was exactly what I needed right now. Not!

"Step aside, Brutus," I told the cat. "This is none of your business."

But Brutus didn't make a move to let me pass. Instead, he walked right up to me and got in my face. "If anyone is getting involved in stuff that isn't his business, it's you, Max. I saw you, you know, spying on Chief Alec and Chase. So that's how you do things in this town, huh? You're Odelia Poole's personal spy. I knew there was a reason she was always getting the best scoops. And now I know her secret. Wait till I tell Chase all about this!"

A chill suddenly settled around the base of my spine. "How are you going to do that, Brutus? You can't talk to your human like I can talk to mine."

Oh, crap. Had I just said that? Bad Max!

He grinned evilly, like Bruce the shark from that fish movie Odelia likes to watch when she's babysitting one of her cousins.

"So you *can* talk to humans," he said slowly. "I thought as much. I only arrived yesterday, but already I've heard the rumors this Odelia Poole person is a little… shall we say weird? And now you've confirmed my suspicions."

"Well, you still can't do anything with that information," I challenged him. My claws were itching to get a piece of his fur, but I restrained myself. I may be big, but that doesn't mean I'm all lean muscle like Brutus and Chase. My bulk mainly consists of, um, well, love handles. Lots and lots of love handles.

"Maybe I can't talk to my human," he conceded, "but I can make your life a lot more difficult. I can prevent you from snooping around and listening to conversations that aren't intended for your spying ears."

Horrified, I cried, "You can't do that!"

"Oh, yes, I can," he said, that nasty grin still firmly in place. He reared up to his full height, puffing up his chest like the nasty bully he was. "Listen up, Max. From now on the police station is off limits to you and your buddies."

"What?! You have no right!"

"Oh, yes, I do. Chase Kingsley is the law in this town now, which, by extension, makes me the law, too. So I can do whatever I want and there's not a thing you can do about it."

"It doesn't work like that! It's not because your human is a cop that you're also one. That's just crazy talk!"

"I can assure you that's exactly how it works, Max," he grunted.

"No, it's not. Harriet's human is a doctor. That doesn't make her capable of performing brain surgery, does it? And, and…" I cast around wildly. "Dooley's human is this town's biggest gossip. That doesn't mean he's a gossip, too. Oh, wait, actually it does. Dooley is a pretty big gossip. But that's neither here nor there. You're not a cop, Brutus. Cats simply can't be cops!"

"Well, you can't, obviously," he scoffed. "You're not trained to uphold the law. I, on the other hand, am. Chase used to be the NYPD's biggest and baddest detective, and I learned a lot from watching him in action."

"That's just a load of—"

"Hey!" Brutus yelled, holding up a warning paw, claws extended. "Watch it, pal. You want me to arrest you for contempt of cop? No? Didn't think so!"

"Contempt of cop? That's not even a thing!"

"I'm sure it is," he assured me, giving his nose a lick.

"Well, I'm sure it's not. You're simply making this up on the spot."

I tried to sidestep the overbearing cat, but he got in my face again, and hissed, "You're not trespassing again, Max. This is your final warning."

"Oh? And what are you going to do about it?" I challenged him, my tail rearing up and puffing up while I arched my back menacingly.

"Don't make me fight you, Max," he said in a low, menacing voice. "You don't want me to hurt you. I'm warning you."

I backed down. What? Have you ever stared into the slitted eyes of the meanest, biggest, nastiest cat you've ever seen? Let me tell you, it's scary!

"This was your final warning, Max," he growled, and casually displayed three sets of razor-sharp claws and gave me a mock punch on the shoulder.

I gulped. Those claws looked very sharp indeed. So I decided not to get into a fight with this cat. I needed to figure out how to deal with him, but brute force wasn't exactly my forte. That was obviously his department.

"Have it your way, Brutus," I finally said.

"Always," he said with a smug smile. "That's something you will learn soon, Max. You and those other furballs that inhabit this stupid town."

"Hampton Cove is not a stupid town!"

He merely grinned, and stalked off in the direction of the police station, presumably to find out what I'd found out.

Still shaking from the adrenaline rushing through my veins, I started heading for the *Hampton Cove Gazette*. Boy, did I have news for Odelia.

ABOUT NIC

Nic Saint is the pen name for writing couple Nick and Nicole Saint. They've penned novels in the romance, cat sleuth, middle grade, suspense, comedy and cozy mystery genres. Nicole has a background in accounting and Nick in political science and before being struck by the writing bug the Saints worked odd jobs around the world (including massage therapist in Mexico, gardener in Italy, restaurant manager in India, and Berlitz teacher in Belgium).

When they're not writing they enjoy Christmas-themed Hallmark movies (whether it's Christmas or not), all manner of pastry, comic books, a daily dose of yoga (to limber up those limbs), and spoiling their big red tomcat Tommy.

www.nicsaint.com

The Kellys

Murder Motel

Death in Suburbia

Emily Stone

Murder at the Art Class

Washington & Jefferson

First Shot

Alice Whitehouse

Spooky Times

Spooky Trills

Spooky End

Spooky Spells

Ghosts of London

Between a Ghost and a Spooky Place

Public Ghost Number One

Ghost Save the Queen

Box Set 1 (Books 1-3)

A Tale of Two Harrys

Ghost of Girlband Past

Ghostlier Things

Charleneland

Deadly Ride

Final Ride

Neighborhood Witch Committee

Witchy Start

Witchy Worries

Witchy Wishes

Saffron Diffley

Crime and Retribution

Vice and Verdict

The B-Team

Once Upon a Spy

Tate-à-Tate

Enemy of the Tates

Ghosts vs. Spies

The Ghost Who Came in from the Cold

Witchy Fingers

Witchy Trouble

Witchy Hexations

Witchy Possessions

Witchy Riches

Box Set 1 (Books 1-4)

The Mysteries of Bell & Whitehouse

One Spoonful of Trouble

Two Scoops of Murder

Three Shots of Disaster

Box Set 1 (Books 1-3)

A Twist of Wraith

A Touch of Ghost

A Clash of Spooks

Made in the USA
Las Vegas, NV
20 December 2022

63743424R00121